DUST BATH
REVIVAL

FERAL SEASONS
- BOOK ONE -

MARIANNE KIRBY

CURIOSITY QUILLS PRESS

A Division of **Whampa, LLC**

P.O. Box 2160

Reston, VA 20195

Tel/Fax: 800-998-2509

http://curiosityquills.com

Cover Art by Eugene Teplitsky

http://eugeneteplitsky.deviantart.com

ISBN 978-1-62007-192-2 (ebook)

ISBN 978-1-62007-196-0 (paperback)

CHAPTER ONE

Wide Town

That was the summer of elbows and angles, learning the geometry of girls' legs crossed at the knees. It was sticky, always salty hot, and a sweet smell tinged the air most nights. The sky hung over us, waiting for something. It was more patient than I was.

The wide-angle mirror outside the door of Wanton's general store—the one that let you see what was coming up behind you and most of the porch and street, too—reflected mostly empty back at me. It was getting on dusk and people were settling in for the short summer night. They were locking their doors, even where there hadn't been a problem for years. Issues were rare enough this far south and east, but Wanton hadn't survived everything it had by being a town that took risks.

And some situations you didn't have to find yourself in real regular to remember how bad things could be. People barred their heavy doors strong and tight every night just in case and counted themselves both smart and lucky.

We still had a long drive back to Aunt Marty's place before we would be safe from the dark, Ben having taken his sweet time, flirting with the girl behind the counter. Laura was closer to my age than his, but she was what Aunt Marty called an early bloomer. Ben was stuck all in her blossom like a pollen drunk bee. I rolled my eyes at it; Laura might toss her hair at him, but I'd heard she was going steady with Rory

Jenkins—and Rory wasn't a man who liked competition, especially from outskirts folks like us.

My reflection wavered as I rocked back and forth on my heels. Sixteen years old and only 5 foot 2 in my bare feet—and I was in my bare feet as much as I could get away with when we were back home even if I was wearing heavy black boots to protect my toes now—and round all over. Short and stout like that teapot song I could vaguely remember singing as a little kid to earn somebody's approval. Probably my mother's. Marty said I was most likely a late starter, but I figured if I was never anything other than solid in the middle and flat-chested, that would be pretty much okay. I wished I was a couple inches taller though, mostly when I needed to reach something on a high shelf. My hair, real dark brown where it wasn't bleached in streaks at the temples from the sun, was all in a tangle down my back. My t-shirt and cut-offs were about as fancy as I ever dressed and dusty as all get out from the truck ride in.

Paved roads didn't make much difference once it got this dry, this scorched. Middle of the season, before what passed for the rains, and everything was gritty.

I nodded at Perkins Gentry where he was giving me the side-eye as he locked up the post office across the street. Everyone must have been in from all over to get their mail for the week.

"You waiting on your brother?"

The dust made everyone suspicious; it had been like this every summer I could remember.

"Yes, sir. He's inside, finishing up. How are you and Ms. Rita?" Being polite made things easier. It wasn't like you got to pick your neighbors, after all. I'd known the Gentrys, and everyone else in town for that matter, since before I had even lived in Wanton—and I'd know them until I died, more than likely. We might live further out than just about anyone, but we were part of the community just the same.

That's how I knew Rita Gentry was recovering from whatever sickness had laid her low and so asking about her would give Perkins a chance to smile. Which he did. Even with the whole of the street between us, I could see his face soften.

"She's doing real well. Much better. You thank your aunt for me, for the menthol rub."

I nodded, offered him a smile of my own. Fair trade. "I'll be sure to pass that on. I know she'll be glad to hear it helped." She would be, too—Marty was always helping people with what she had, what she could find, and what she could otherwise get hold of. Helping each other was one thing that kept us all safe, out on the edges of town's security.

Perkins returned my nod, relaxed and friendly now, and finished locking up. He whistled as he headed off home, and I scuffed my boot sole across the planks of the store's porch. I'd waited long enough, given Ben plenty of time to put on his damn charm show. I stuck my head in through the open doorway. Flies were the least of people's concerns when it was starting to get on to dusk.

"Hurry up, Ben. You know Marty'll worry." I stepped inside and looked around more out of habit than the expectation anything would be new. The general store was where we got most of the supplies we either needed quick or didn't feel like arranging for ourselves. Every other week, a heavy armored cargo truck made the long haul from the railway depot to restock the shelves. Food we couldn't grow locally (mostly lettuces, when we were being honest instead of lazy), batteries, oil, radio parts, beauty products. The selection made me dizzy when I was little. Now I mostly just wanted to grab what was on the list and head out—there were more interesting things to do than shop.

My brother was leaning on his elbows on the counter, bent at the hip like it didn't put his ass right out in the air. Damn ridiculous, is what it was. Laura must not have minded, hunched over the counter with him, smiling her pink smile and honest-to-goodness giggling. I knew she made her lips shine like that with petroleum jelly. She just wanted people to look at her mouth. But did Ben care?

"I'd hate to get you in trouble." She pouted at him.

I frowned. Ben just smiled bigger though.

"And I hate to leave you here without any company. We'll be fine getting back. But what about you?" Ben slowly straightened and shot me a quick look of annoyance before easing his face back into its lines of concern.

"I do a good job taking care of myself, Benjamin Goodness, don't you worry. Besides, Rory's coming over at closing so he can take me home." Laura delivered that last line like a knife to the ribs, and Ben responded by rubbing at his side like he'd felt it slip in right where it hurt the most.

I was just about ready to throw up on both of them if they didn't cut it out. Laura was pretty enough, but she was a snake when it came to romance. I stomped over to the counter. "Is our stuff ready?"

Laura made a face at me and gestured at the bags and whatnot by Ben's feet—I hadn't even noticed, I was so riled up from waiting. "You're all set, Hank. Unless I can sell you a brush?" She called me by my nickname, but there wasn't any fondness in how she pronounced it. Laura had never approved of me—or my rat's nest. I didn't much care, so I made a face right back at her.

Ben, oblivious and taking the opportunity to look right down her blouse, just picked up the bags and gave her one last smile even as he elbowed me in the chest, nudging me back toward the door. "Well, now, you make sure Rory takes care of you, treats you as best he can."

It was mean—I knew that even as I did it—but I couldn't resist making a barfing noise. It was a pretty good one—Laura paled and put a hand to her mouth.

She'd always had a weak stomach when it came to puke. She blinked and found her flirtation again where she'd dropped it on the counter. "I'll keep that in mind, Ben. You drive safe."

She didn't have a word for me, but I was already out the door ahead of my brother and halfway to the truck before she could have said anything anyway. She was a grade ahead of me at the old school when we'd both been going, and she'd always been a priss and a snob. The first day we met during recess, she'd knocked me down and then pretended she didn't know what I was crying about when the teacher had come asking.

I had a long damn memory was all.

Climbing up and over the tailgate of our old Ford, I grabbed the bags Ben handed to me. We'd stocked up on a few things, light bulbs, toilet paper, and some cucumbers to replace the crop we'd just lost to fire.

Lightning had started it. At least, that was what Marty'd been telling the neighbors. If she'd spent most of that morning muttering to the backs of our heads that there was something wrong with that field, something just plain wrong, that wasn't meant for anyone else's ears. Marty was just a little touched sometimes. But either way, she still had plans to put up pickles so we had a bushel of cucumbers just the same.

Bags and baskets stowed, Ben gestured for me to lean closer. I did— and he flicked my ear.

"Damn it, Hank, why you got to be like that with Laura?"

I slapped at him, used the leverage of my perch in the truck bed to push at him until he stumbled, laughing. "You're such an idiot. She's going steady with Rory, and he'll come looking for you and trouble both if he hears you're messing with her. You know she's just stirring it up with him."

The shake of his head cut me off. "You don't understand. So you just hush up and let me have my fun." He snorted when I opened my mouth, then pulled open the driver's side door. "You riding up front or what?"

I set my jaw, ground my teeth in aggravation until I could hear them squeak. "I'll ride in back."

It wasn't a smart choice—the sun was already fading and the truck bed wasn't real protected or even all that comfortable. I could sit on the rolled-up tarp we'd never gotten around to putting anywhere else, but there wasn't any place to hide. We could stand to lose a bag of light bulbs or produce if it came down to it, but I wouldn't be so easy to replace if anything happened.

Ben must have been thinking something similar because he squinted up at the sky, a hand raised with his palm flat to ward off the glare of looking straight at the low sun, then looked back at me. "You sure?" He stepped one foot up into the truck, ready to lift himself into the seat. His other foot stayed planted in the dirt; it would leave a solid footprint. "I wouldn't mind the company."

One of these days I'd be able to stay mad at Ben. But it just wasn't that day. I sighed, played at being put upon, but climbed down out of the back of the truck and made my way to the passenger door. I brushed my hands off on the seat of my shorts, casual. Honestly, I was glad he'd given me the excuse to change my mind. The door hinges squealed when I hauled the door open, then again when I slammed it. The noise was loud in the quiet of the street. "I guess I can sit up here. But just for your sake."

Ben never could hold a grudge either, at least not with me—maybe that was where I got it. And with me having spent so much damn time in the passenger seat of my big brother's pickup as he raced it down dirt roads, with the radio droning on about the weather and the Reborn and wars in other places, by the time we were hitting the town limits, we were back to our usual selves, him picking at my lack of sociability and me calling him a butterfly. The radio static filled in all the gaps.

It wasn't that I weren't social. I liked people. Particular people. I just didn't have any patience for Laura and her clean, soft hands that never did anything but take money or write notes in the store ledger. I didn't care about her disapproval—she didn't think I was much of a girl and she wasn't even wrong that I didn't know anything about makeup or doing my hair—but that didn't mean I liked dealing with her attitude either. It was easier to just avoid her and her little group, all of them reeking of Florida Water and going out of their way to poke at me and make me feel stupid. And ugly. They were real convinced I was ugly. Mostly that meant avoiding town, staying on the outskirts with everyone else like us who couldn't handle living behind so many walls and fences.

Our town didn't have a sharp border so much as it kind of trickled out in a staggered series of tall fences around people's little plots of lands. The paved state road ran in one side and out the other, parallel to the old train tracks—the train didn't come to us anymore. If anyone wanted out or through, they took the road, and it was the safest way anyway; the state troopers patrolled it, at least during the day. Traveling at night was a bad idea for anybody—badges weren't effective against everything in the dark.

There were places outside the fences, all built up with good, strong walls: a gas station that catered to further-out folks like us, a roadside stall selling sea shells to the few vacationers who still came for the warmth in winter, a stable for day trips on horseback, and a bunch of mechanics—they could fix cars or tractors, anything that had manufactured moving parts. All of them were locked up against the dusk. It came around sooner once you were outside the tightly packed buildings and houses that made townies feel secure, had bolder shadows than dared show up under the electric streetlight that always flashed yellow. You could sometimes get someone to open up a locked door but it didn't pay much to bank on it; you might as well have been banking on a dirt crop in Oklahoma. All empty graves and promises no one had been able to keep.

The wind picked up, and we swerved over the middle line in the road a little bit—but since we were the only ones on it, we were good. I held onto the dashboard as best I could. Ben gripped the steering wheel even tighter once we turned off the smoothness of the pavement and onto the dirt of the side road back to our place. The dirt had been packed down into ruts that showed the pattern of our tire treads. The path itself wound long and snakelike back to the house across a couple acres of Marty's property. When we actually got rain, the whole thing flooded in a flash and then slowly drained out, sand over limestone. Nothing solid in Florida, Marty always said.

This weather wasn't coming up on rain, though. It was all heat lightning and wind. The thunder would pick up soon, too, so much noise and crash. It would scare the rabbits into hiding, make them nervous and hard to hunt for the next few days. There'd be just long enough for them to calm down, and then we'd get another just like this one. That was the way things worked.

The tires sunk in deep where the wind had blown the sand into the miniature dunes, made the truck sluggish. It wasn't white sand—I'd heard they had that at the beach, but ours was grey, dirt grey and super fine. It got in everywhere, especially between my toes and fingers. When the heat made me sweat, I wound up with black tracks across my palms and the soles of my feet. Marty wouldn't let me in the house until I'd hosed myself off on the back porch.

I could tell the steering was mushy by the wrinkle of concentration on Ben's forehead. Too easy, in this kind of weather, to get blown right off the road and into the ditch—and then we'd have to hoof it home through the twilight. It wasn't a bad walk, as a general rule—and if everything could be counted on to stay the way it was, I would have been fine doing it. But if we got a stranger or a Reborn wandering around, well. Gambling was a foolish hobby from what I'd heard about it. I had better things to do with my pennies. And, still, I reckoned as I pulled the sweaty collar of my t-shirt away from my neck in the hopes of catching some of the moving air against my moist skin, it was a damn shame humans just weren't meant any longer to run around in the shade of the evening. It was awfully pretty when it was just going dark.

"What are you mooning about over there?" Ben still had both hands fighting the wheel but he laughed over at me, scrunched up in the corner between the seat back and the door. The radio static had given way to a weather report, all thunder and no rain though there was bound to be some heat lightning.

I wrinkled my nose at him. "Who says I'm mooning?" Childish, to wonder about things you can't change, Marty always said. And I ought to be old enough to know better. It's hard, though, having read all of Marty's real old books, the ones printed before things changed. Pure science fiction these days, the idea of midnight garden parties, but I still dreamed. There were paragraphs and paragraphs about moonlit walks and the starlit sky. My embarrassment made me a bit snappier than I'd have been otherwise. "Could be I'm just sitting here waiting on someone worth talking to."

The hurt flashed across, a bird-fast expression, just like I would have predicted if I'd stopped to think before opening my damn mouth. Now I felt guilty. Ben always hid his hurt quick. When we were younger, he didn't have such a knack for pretending, but as his little chat with Laura had proved, Ben had gotten a lot better at putting on a face when he felt like it. Hell, maybe that was why he talked to her in the first place: practice. Well, practice and her cleavage.

Ben was always so concerned with being the man of the family, an apology would wear on his feelings and be worse than the original offense, probably. I held my tongue. The radio switched to the news, what there was of it. The fighting trudged on in Europe, had dragged out for twice my lifetime while America stayed at home and took care of its own. We'd learned, Marty said, from that business with the Great War.

I struggled for another topic. "You think there was really anything wrong with those cukes?" I knew what I thought, but Ben had been so tight-lipped on the subject, his lips might as well have been glued together.

That got me a sideways glance, accompanied by a swerve until Ben swore and got our old beast straightened back out. "You mean before or after they got lit on fire?"

My snort made him crack a smile, at least. But he sobered right up.

"I went out and looked at them last week. They were growing in and looked about ready to pick to me. But..." He sighed. "They were all bunched up, growing real thick in the middle of the field, close together, almost on top of each other. That ain't how they were planted."

It shouldn't have sounded like much. But Marty had us plant things, every single time, in neat and tidy rows. I learned more about algebra and geometry from figuring out how many rows we could fit in a field than I ever did down at the school. We'd done basic math there, but no one was even sure we'd need it.

We were about a half mile from driving past the dark and empty field where the cukes had been, and my stomach felt funny at the thought of it, like it was trying to hold on to a fist that wanted to reach up my throat and into my mouth. I yawned, stretched, tried to ignore it.

"You think she spilled the seeds when she was planting and they grew in funny or something?" It didn't seem likely, but it was the best I could do.

Ben chewed on his lower lip. It was a bad habit I shared; we did it when we were unsure about something, nervous about giving an answer that might not be correct. He held on to his words until we were halfway past the field.

Then he slammed on the brakes; the truck shuddered and slid in the sand, and I grabbed on to whatever I could. He flung his door open and made a run for the field, slipping and hopping over what was left of the rows. Green vines smoldered more than they burnt.

"What the blue hell are you doing?" I shouted after him, but the wind took my voice, tossed it right back into the cab of the truck.

He was hurrying in any event, grabbed something, then came tear-assing back. He tossed whatever it was at me and climbed in, slammed his door behind him. Sat with both hands on the wheel for a minute, panting and white-knuckled.

My mouth was still open to shout at him. But I turned the thing he'd thrown at me over in my hands. It was charred but still recognizable. A red baseball cap, torn up and filthy with mud and water and soot. It looked like something had done a number on it before it'd been set on fire.

I stared at it, dropped it on the bench seat between us like it still had the power to burn me. The sky was getting darker, and we were just sitting there, but just then, moving was beyond us.

Rose Gordon, the minister's daughter, almost always wore a red baseball cap, with her long brown ponytail swinging through the hole in the back. I'd envied her damn ponytail more than once because it was smooth and glossy. She'd been wearing that hat, her daddy told everyone, when she went missing more than a month before. No one had seen hide nor hair of her for going on six weeks—which wasn't the longest we'd gone without going into town, but people weren't surprised about that sort of thing with us; it was expected we were going to be a little funny and standoffish. Rose lived right up against the fences. Her father swore the Reborn were angels walking among us, proof of divine intervention on earth. He even, I'd heard it whispered on some lazy Sunday afternoons, slept with his doors unlocked.

That would have made it real easy for Rose to sneak out. Her daddy wasn't mean, but he didn't like boys sniffing around, especially David

Stanton, the boy she'd been seeing every day after school. David lived almost as far out as we did, so no one had really counted him missing—but to my mind, they'd probably holed up somewhere together or maybe even caught a train north.

A torn-up baseball cap didn't prove me wrong. But it made that fist in my stomach tighten up and struggle.

Ben didn't have to say anything—the sick look on his face felt like a cracked mirror version of mine. I avoided his eyes, pale and staring straight ahead, then jumped when the radio gave another burst of static before settling back into Homer Stin's recorded voice telling us to be careful of lightning and Reborn walking ahead of the wind, the standard storm warning repeating and repeating.

The truck lurched again when Ben put it in gear and eased us back on our way. I turned the sound down but not off and looked out the window as we bumped along, slower than I'd have liked after that kind of discovery, across Marty's land.

Owning land made a difference. Property was still worth something. It meant you didn't have to be as dependent on the armored trucks, on waiting for the fresh and preserved food coming down from all points north. You had options, even if one of them was just selling up and living off the proceeds for as long as you could manage.

It also meant that you were isolated. You had to stomach living risky. We'd mostly avoided any real trouble. There were regular sightings, but seeing at a distance wasn't the same thing as coming up on a Reborn all up close and personal. Every ten years or so, Marty said, someone from the outside of town would get sick of the place, pack up and move, riding the rails if they could catch them or—for the daring— the roads to find a new place to be. Those folks always took oranges with them—everyone knew citrus protected you from turning.

Something in the vitamin C, the old folks claimed.

We kept on down the road, the radio giving squarely back over to static when whoever ran the station thought people were adequately warned. Staying quiet the rest of the way back to our dinner was not just easy. It was the only thing we could do.

CHAPTER TWO

Big Tent

I f there was one thing Marty believed in, it was getting up early to get our damn chores done. Which is why I threw the locks and was out the door as soon as the first light touched the sky. I liked it early in the day anyway—nothing nearly so dark as the night I glimpsed through the high, narrow slits of the window in our living room, but something different from the blaze of full sun at midday or even the shade of cloudy weather.

It took a while for the sun to finish rising. The air was still cool, and even the dirt under my bare toes felt calm and clean. Even though it was, by definition, dirty.

We'd had a cow once, when I'd been real little. Now we had goats. Marty claimed the milk made better cheese and it didn't upset her stomach. I wouldn't have argued anyway. The people we knew with cows told us the beasts took up more time and space and energy—none of that sounded appealing. Ben said I was just lazy; I said cows were just boring. And I got up before he did anyway.

It was one of our usual morning squabbles; Ben finally headed up to the goat pen, still rubbing the sleep out of his eyes, while I headed for the chicken coop. The metal building was surrounded by a high, chain-link fence; it protected the little grassy chicken yard. The shiny curls of razor wire on top caught the light and glittered like something fancy.

But when I got closer, the gate looked crooked on its hinges. Feathers were scattered all over the enclosure. Another step, and my eyes focused on the sad little pile of tail feathers by the back corner fence post. They were most of them clean, but slick dried blood still dotted a few of them.

None of us had heard anything in the night—not that we would. The house was built solid. Even if something broke the few windows and tried to come in after us, the door between the living room and the rest of the house was strong enough to balance out the risk from the luxury of glass. Even so, we had a rule: if you heard anything in the night, you woke everyone else up. That way we'd all have an equal chance.

The gate was sort of closed, and I'd have believed someone was out rustling chickens if not for that pile of dinner leavings—it was like someone had used the butt end of the chicken like the handle of a drumstick.

It caught me off guard as being damn funny. Because chickens had legs—they literally had drumsticks. And if you were going to use a handle to eat a chicken, why wouldn't you just hold them by the legs? Though Marty and Ben both liked chicken feet. Maybe that's what had happened—a rustler with a taste for chicken feet.

A hysterical giggle bubbled up and out of my mouth before I could catch it and stuff it back down. I coughed to cover it, hide it even from myself. And then I felt bad, badder than bad—we had a lot of birds, but I liked them all, and now at least one... My feet carried me to the door of the coop; my good sense stopped me short. Rushing in where I couldn't see wouldn't have been the dumbest thing I'd ever done, but it would have been pushing my luck.

My breath filled my chest up, kept me still and silent to listen. Nothing. The chickens would have been kicking up a fuss if there were something inside with them—unless they were all dead. I crouched low and walked on my knees to the door, down low and hopefully less of a target for anything conceivably waiting on the other side. The door creaked when it cracked open enough for me to inch my face around so I could see.

The rest of the birds were bunched up against the back wall, huddled together. Still scared, it looked like. They wouldn't be laying, that was for certain. I clucked at them, as reassuring as I could be without being a chicken myself. My knees barely tolerated me standing up; my head swam with relief even so. We'd skip our eggs at breakfast this morning or use some of the excess from yesterday stored in Marty's little cooler, but I needed to make sure my girls were okay.

A quick headcount showed two birds missing. They had probably been roosting out in the yard because it was so hot, even at night. Most of the feathers outside could be the result of a bunch of panicking hens rushing around like their fool heads had been cut off; there was just that one tidy little pile to tell me something bad had happened. The other chicken had probably been carted off for later, though there was no telling when later would have been. Unless she'd been eaten with her tail feathers intact. Neither scenario was precisely reassuring.

"Hank. Hey, Hank, come back out here." Ben's voice sounded far away—the insulated coop walls muffled the sound.

I clucked at the hens one more time before backing out into the morning.

"Something got in with the birds last night." That was more important than saying hello. Ben didn't look upset or even a little bit mussed, just awake and focused on something, so nothing had happened to the goats. He always managed to stay tidy during morning chores somehow. Meanwhile, I hadn't even scattered the feed and already smelled like ammonia—my reward for kneeling in chicken shit. Stupid chickens. I sank my hand into the sack and tossed the seed out so the cluckers would find it when they finally ventured into the yard to forage for grasshoppers.

Ben waved a hand, dismissed my news. "Look at the road." He pointed up the drive leading to the house—where the brightly painted panel trucks were bouncing over the ruts, flags flying from antennas and music blaring from a radio in at least one of them. I squinted, but the lettering on the lead hood was too faded to make out at a distance, even if the colors glared against the gray sky.

"What's going on?"

We got visitors every now and then. Sometimes it would be someone who had pulled off the highway—they wound up on our front porch with a flat tire or a busted radiator or something that Ben would fix up as best he could to get them close enough to town for actual help. If he couldn't, he'd fire up the truck and carry the visitor into town himself. He'd do it extra fast if there were a pretty girl involved.

But there hadn't ever been anything like the caravan pulling up in our front yard like it was no business at all to organize that kind of group. And we never got strangers this early in the day—in fact, I couldn't even think of where they'd have been coming from that they'd reached us just as the sun was finishing up clearing the horizon. There wasn't any place within that kind of distance. "They must've driven all through the night." It was a quick whisper out the side of my mouth, and Ben shot me a scattered look before he nodded. That meant he hadn't thought of that himself.

"You go get Marty, Hank." He was straightening up, deepening his voice a little bit. He was going to play at being the grown man he really mostly was.

It frightened me a little. Not because he'd never done it before, but because, for a second, I was grateful that he did—then I scrambled for the house, feed sack still clutched in my fist.

I didn't even stop to wipe my shoes off first, and the door banged loud behind me. "Marty? Hey, Aunt Marty?" There was really only one place she was likely to be at this time of morning. Marty got up earlier than either me or Ben, and I wasn't real sure what she did when it was still dark out. But when we were done with our chores, there was always breakfast, ready and waiting. I headed for the kitchen.

Marty still had a wooden spoon in her hand, but she was already turned toward me. "What's the ruckus?"

"Strangers—in trucks. They're pulling up in the yard now." I almost blurted out about the chickens, too, but whatever (and I knew what that was, even though I didn't want to admit it) had gotten the birds was gone, while the strangers were parking in our front patch as we spoke. That was the higher priority. It still didn't spur Marty to move very quickly.

Her nod was curt, though, and she tried to hand me her spoon. "You stir the grits while I go see what they want."

She gave me a look when I stepped away, my hands behind my back. "You know I'll just burn them." I had yet to manage much success in the kitchen, no matter how much Marty tried to pass her knowledge on. Besides, I didn't want to be stuck at the stove when there were more interesting things going on—we hadn't had strangers of any sort in over a year. If she insisted, I'd just watch through the window over the sink, and the grits would still be a ruined lump by the time she came back.

Marty seemed to know it; she thumped the spoon down on the counter and pulled the pot off the burner. The grits could sit cold for a little while without too much injury. "Let's go satisfy that curiosity of yours then." She sounded put out, but letting me get out of a direct instruction like that was about as indulgent as Marty ever got. I shifted my weight from foot to foot as she opened the pantry and pulled out the sawed-off shotgun she kept there for emergencies.

Then she nodded at me to lead the way.

We went through the formal entry. I held the wooden door, heavy and thick, open for Marty, and she kept the shotgun leaning casually against her hip. Ben stood at the base of the porch steps, old railroad ties that looked like they'd been there forever, with his eyes on the two men stepping down out of the lead truck onto the scrub grass of our little front yard.

The strangers wore collared shirts, button-ups with short sleeves, tucked into belted trousers. They had short hair; in fact, they both had the same haircut, it looked like. Maybe their barber traveled with them and only knew how to do the one style. They were taller than Ben, which meant they were well taller than me, and lanky like they'd been on the road so long they'd outrun regular meals. The blond one was smiling. The darker one looked older, more lines on his face, serious. He didn't have the same smile lines that Marty did though. He was younger than her or he'd just never taken to smiling at people.

"Morning. What can I help you gentlemen with?" Marty's voice was strong and loud enough to carry to where they stood by the hood of their truck. "Y'all got names?"

"Yes, ma'am," the younger smiled even harder. "I'm Leon Putnam, and this is Seymour Oleander. We were just stopping by to ask after some directions."

"The road signs are pretty clear around these parts." Ben sounded like he didn't trust them. He kept on using that grown-up voice he'd turned on me. And he did have a point. The green highway signs, put up by the government, named towns and distances, how far you had to go before you got safe.

"Well, yes, they certainly are." Leon's lips stretched tight over his teeth for a moment.

My guess was he didn't like being challenged. "What I meant was, we were hoping to inquire if you've got an empty field we might be able to take advantage of. For a fair price, of course."

Before Ben could respond, Marty barked out a laugh. "What are you selling, Mr. Putnam? What's your Mr. Oleander over there want with my field?" I was willing to bet she still looked real casual to our visitors, if you didn't go by the whiteness of her knuckles as she gripped the shotgun's stock.

The two men traded a look. They weren't good at hiding much. I took a step forward from slightly behind Marty, another one, right up to the porch rail that passed as a bench when we were enjoying the late afternoon some days. The older one, Seymour, moved like that had been an invitation and stuck his hand out for Ben to shake. Ben let it hang there a minute, then fished his handkerchief out of his back pocket to wipe his palm clean like he wasn't in any hurry. He gripped Seymour's hand and they shook.

We had to be courteous to them now, if nothing else. Not like we wouldn't have been otherwise. But still.

"Ma'am, we're not selling anything other than refreshments. The rest of our offerings are free to the public, for their spiritual welfare." He addressed himself to Marty, but looked at all three of us, from one to the next, like he wanted to be sure not to insult anybody. "My ministry does take in the occasional donation, but that's up to the will of the people's good hearts."

That sounded like a load of manure if I'd ever heard one. He was a preacher, and he wanted to set up shop on our land. I must have made a face because he turned that solemn expression on me and cocked his head to one side.

"Now, young ma'am, I can tell you aren't a believer. But every one of us comes to God in our own time and way. I'm just looking for an empty plot to help those that are interested in this time and place." He didn't try to smile, which was probably for the best. Those unlined cheeks might've cracked under the strain. But even without a smile, he managed to look like he had something blazing inside that he was holding back.

It made me nervous. I looked to Ben, who was frowning, and then to Marty.

It wasn't a frown on Marty's lined face. It was more like she was doing math in her head and concentrating on carrying the two. She lowered the shotgun until the butt of it rested on the porch. "And what's a reasonable price?"

The cucumber field was empty. It was right up near the road, and there was plenty of space for a traveling preacher and his tents without anything else getting trampled. I tried to weigh Marty's dislike of organized religion against her mercenary streak—Marty was quick to take our pocket money back from us when we were foolish enough to bet against her—but just when I thought she was going to send this pair of fools on their way, she chuckled, low and complicated.

Seymour may have been a preacher, but it looked like he was a money man, too. He knew he'd caught her interest. "I wouldn't insult a lady by negotiating with her. You tell Mr. Putnam what's reasonable, and I trust that you'll operate with Christian charity in your heart."

That was probably his first big mistake.

His second was telling us, once he'd finally come up on the porch and sat down, leaving Leon to cool his heels by the truck, that we were welcome anytime to come by and participate in his meetings. Marty shook her head and declined right away, but Ben caught my eye; we just needed to find the right opportunity. At the moment, though, we needed to get on with our chores. Marty sent us off on our way and gave Ben the benefit of a swat to the back of his head. She was a hard woman, Marty.

By the time the chicken yard was all sparkling and the gate once again sat snug and safe on its hinges, the birds had come on out of the coop. They were scratching around in the dirt and grass, clucking like gossipy old men when they found an insect or bit of feed. I clucked back at them until the morning felt almost normal. My near panic earlier seemed like an overreaction when I latched the gate tight behind me.

Our chores seemed to take twice as long after our late start at most of them. When Ben and I headed in for breakfast, Seymour's men had just started working the field, trading shouts and pointing at empty spaces while the trucks all drove around and tried to stay out of everyone's way. The grits were a little lumpy, like Marty had been too distracted to stir them enough when she came back inside, but complaining about the food was always a bad idea—a sure ticket to an empty belly at the next meal.

Seymour didn't hang up his shingle that first day, though there was a lot of hammering and general noise. A couple of the trucks took off toward town in the afternoon, and Ben directed my attention back to the tomatoes we were supposed to be picking clean of caterpillars before I could get too nosy. The next day brought a few attendees, mostly other folks from the outskirts like us, curious enough to stick their heads in the tents—and they mostly left as quick as they saw what was in there. It wasn't until dusk that I realized Seymour and his crew weren't shutting down for the night; they kept their lights burning and their music playing. Ben and I vied for position at the window over the kitchen sink that gave us a little view of the action before Marty yelled at us and sent us to bed behind the big door. She hadn't done that since Ben had set a bunch of grass snakes loose in the living room one day when we had just come to live with her.

I rushed out the third morning, partly to see to the chickens, who had all gotten back to normal even though the humans were riled up, but also to make sure the strangers had survived the dark. A straggly line of sleepy people was winding out of what had to be a cook tent judging by the plates in their hands. I'd almost worked up the nerve to sneak up closer, when one of the hens pecked at my big toe and my concentration was busted.

"Here, you old savage thing." I dumped a handful of feed on her head just to watch her flap around. When I looked up again, Ben was coming out of the goat pen and it was time to move on to our other chores.

But the tent pulled and caught at my attention, no matter how hard I worked myself. After lunch, during the high heat of the day when we usually gathered inside before Marty took a little laydown, I kicked my leg forward to make the porch swing move a little bit and watched. More folks milled about there than yesterday, more cars parked, too. The noise was quiet, but it was steady, just a low, regular hum of electricity and a crowd crammed all in together.

There wasn't really any conscious decision that led me to wander down off the porch. I didn't say to myself, self, let's walk on out and be careful not to step on any sand spurs. It was like something was pulling me, my curiosity getting the better of me until I found myself at the edges of the unguarded main tent, peeking in like a fool looking for fairies around every corner.

Seymour was on his knees, his shirt still somehow crisp and pristine in the heat and humidity. He wasn't even sweating. I didn't know how he was doing it until I looked to the left and then to the right; there were electric fans hooked up to blow steady on him and him alone.

It struck me as deeply unfair for a hot minute, but then they probably couldn't haul around a large enough generator to keep everyone cool. Maybe all they had the juice for was those two teeny things. And the breeze did seem keep Seymour looking nice and cool, like someone who ought to be listened to. Everyone else was kind of wilted. Even the feather on Elton Mather's hat was drooping.

A motion, just a small gesture of fingers, caught my eye and I nodded to Elenor Sminten. When she twitched her hand at me again to take the empty seat next to her, I sighed in relief, then edged in under the tent flap on quiet feet. It'd been a while since I'd seen the inside of a church; the inside of a tent probably had different rules but anything religious probably meant I should keep my mouth shut just about all the way.

Everyone was near silent, and for a minute there I was afraid I'd come in on some sort of weird prayer where everybody kept their eyes open. But then Seymour raised his bent head, standing up in a single motion. I hadn't expected him to be so graceful.

"My new friends, welcome. The terrible sun of Satan's power beats down on us, but here we can find the shade of God's love, the cool refreshment of God's power." Seymour didn't raise his voice like the minister in town. That was Rose Gordon's daddy, and I brushed that thought off real quick like someone was going to pick it out of my head if it stayed there too long. Everybody hung on Seymour's words, and you could have heard a pin drop. The lack of volume didn't hurt his sense of conviction none.

He kept up in the same vein, and I let my attention wander even as my eyes stayed mostly forward. It was a trick I'd learned in school when I wanted to daydream; I'd gotten paddled plenty for rushing through my work, turning it in sloppy so I could think about anything but where I was and what I was doing.

The crowd—congregation, more like—wasn't big. While I recognized almost all the faces, there was a man in a suit who didn't belong. He didn't look to feel the heat of the air in the tent any more than Seymour did, kept himself crisp and pressed and creased somehow without the benefit of fans. He held still when all the other bodies started moving. It began with a little bit of swaying; it got faster as the rhythm of Seymour's words steadied, as his fist started a percussive pounding on the makeshift podium he stood next too—just a couple of stacked up crates. And then, just when Seymour fell silent, old Jelly Little, who I'd never seen do anything other than sit in front of the ticket office at the train depot and chew tobacco, stood up and opened his mouth.

Jelly Little wasn't really old—probably not even as old as Marty. But he looked like someone had dropped a rock on his face. Maybe that had really happened—no one was real sure and Jelly didn't talk about it. Didn't talk at all. I wasn't sure if he couldn't, so I turned to get myself a better look.

The voice that trickled out between his parched lips was a rasp, a rough sound scraping against sensitive eardrums. I couldn't even make out what he was saying. But the reactions of the other townies were clear enough. They stood up until one of them fell down, flat out on her back on the dirt floor with a joyful cry of Hallelujah.

Seymour himself rushed forward with a canteen of what was probably water. Jelly turned his head away, but Seymour grabbed the man by the chin and forced the spout between Jelly's teeth until he had to drink or drown. Jelly sputtered and thrashed, but all of a sudden he seized up and then started drinking deep. When Seymour finally pulled the canteen away, a little gasp escaped me. I couldn't hear so much as my own heartbeat over Seymour's shout. Jelly's lips were wet and pink, and the man was crying, tears tracking mud on his dusty face.

I felt ashamed of myself for watching that. Nobody had ever sobbed their eyes out at the church in town. Minister Gordon had never cradled anybody against his shoulder. He'd never started up a hymn with his own strong voice.

The song was something I'd never heard, kind of like a lullaby. Jelly shook for a while, calming down, but the knot in my stomach grew. The man in the suit was just where he'd been the whole time, still as anything, watching. I needed to get back to my chores. No one paid me any mind anyway, so I kept myself to myself and edged out of the tent.

Telling Marty any of this was bound to be a mistake. Maybe Ben could help me make heads or tails, once he got back in from his afternoon job of delivering papers around.

But Ben made himself scarce the rest of the day. And by that evening, the tent still had a crowd—almost as big as that afternoon, and the shouting reached all to the house. It didn't sound dangerous, but it didn't make any sense to me. What was the point to all the racket? The dirt road was narrowed by cars pulled off to the side, skirting the edges of our other fields; Marty had glared at that but said nothing. Seymour must have been plenty generous with his fair price. I held my tongue, the moment to tell my brother what I'd seen lost to exhaustion.

Marty had narrowed her eyes at me when she woke up from her nap. She'd kept her silence, then piled those damn chores on me faster than ever. Then wouldn't you know it, we were locking up every night.

By the time it was nearing full dark the next Saturday night, I could have told you what time it was by the kind of sound that traveled from Seymour's tent over air, shimmering in the heat. But I had yet to creep back over. Tired and filthy with a hard day's work, I slipped in the front door and bolted it behind me for the night. When I flopped down next to Ben on the couch, though, Marty wasn't there.

CHAPTER THREE

Like An Old Time Revival

Marty hadn't been around much. Not even for me to tell her about that morning with the chickens. It sat uneasy in my belly, didn't feel like we were really safe if she didn't know. Marty had always kept us safe, and one way she did that was by knowing. I needed to put my back into it, even if it meant interrupting and telling her over breakfast—a surefire way to catch hell.

"She's gone to bed early. Said her stomach's sour from all the noise." Ben brushed it off like it was an insignificant thing, and maybe it was.

I knew what he was getting at so I didn't answer, just went to my room and changed into jeans, put on my boots to protect my feet.

Back in the living room, Ben was ready, too. We headed out through the backdoor instead of the front, and Ben closed it behind us with a key.

I hadn't been outside at night before, at least not that I could really remember. I had a handful of vague memories, though, cool air and a breeze, that made me think my parents had taken us out before they died. But Marty had never so much as unlocked the door once the sun was full down without some kind of good reason.

There weren't a lot of good reasons. As quiet and regular as our lives were, we still knew it was dangerous. I spared some thought for that red ball cap and for the missing chickens. We were in for a world of trouble if Marty got wind of us sneaking out and going wandering. And she probably would; neither of us had yet successfully pulled one over on her. I reckoned Ben would deal with the fallout when the time came. It was his idea, after all.

Everything looked different with the sun down. The moon hung bright and heavy and there were stars just starting to peek out. It wasn't entirely dark—there was enough light to see things in a weird kind of black and white, like a moving picture or a photograph. Even so, there was something unfriendly about the ditches and fence posts. Something unwelcoming in the way the flat, open fields stretched out. Like they were naked and I peeking at them through a shaded window. The night wanted its privacy and me and Ben were just peeping tomcats.

I shivered, a nervous waver of my shoulders, before I squared my back and took off after Ben, up the road those trucks had come down. He shortened his stride so I could catch up; then, together, we footed it the rest of the way up to the field that even before Seymour rolled up had already been causing us nothing but worry.

The noise got louder, then separated into distinct voices as we got closer. The tent was full from what I could see, more townies than I would have expected to brave the night. Two men dressed like Seymour the last time I saw him, shirt sleeves and belts all clean and pressed, hung around the edges of the crowd spaced every couple of yards, keeping their eyes on everything. One of them caught my eye, nodded, and gestured for us to go into the tent, but Ben and I loitered for a minute, still taking it in.

The metal folding chairs set in such neat rows during my daytime visit were scattered everywhere, like the throng under the tent had disarranged any kind of order with just the press and flex of their bodies. I knew these folks, they were good town folks, but I'd never seen them like this.

Seymour himself stood at the mouth of the tent, in front of a pulpit he'd probably started out preaching behind. It was nicer than the stack of boxes he'd had the other day. Now, though, he was shirtless and sweating, those fans not doing near enough, and he still wasn't smiling.

Instead, his mouth was open wide, his lips red, as he raised his voice and shouted about being born again in God's spirit.

The words didn't make a whole lot of sense. But hiding out around the entrance wasn't anything I felt like doing now that we'd come this far, not with the night time so close beyond the open sides of the tent. Not even with guards posted. I stepped past Ben, elbowed him in the side as I moved around him. And then I was stumbling in the midst of a crowd.

I was pushed and pulled on all sides—there weren't any hands grabbing at me, but bodies swayed, arms flailed. Through a momentary gap in the press of it all, I saw a girl I knew—Lisa Macintyre, my age, we'd braided each other's hair during recess— swoon back into the arms of Terrence Little, Jelly's big strong son with his mother's dark skin, who worked as a mechanic on the outskirts of the other side of town. He held her gently, kept her up off the floor while her eyes rolled back in her head. Then a twirl of color filled my eyes, and it was all Laura from the store, Ben's Laura even though she wasn't really Ben's at all, dancing with her snake hips and her long bare arms up over her head.

It made me blush, just watching it. Made my chest ache, too, even though I didn't like her because she was still beautiful. More beautiful than Jenny, who had let me kiss her for the first time at the last town picnic—and who all I could do was hope wasn't in this tent with all these people and this strangeness. I managed to look away from Laura's dance, searched for Ben with something close to a frantic impulse. When my eyes found him, a still and stable height in the middle of the swirl, he was staring, fixated on Laura. He'd forgotten I was even there. I might as well be alone.

He worked his way forward, toward her, and the crowd didn't stand in his way. He reached an arm around Laura's waist and pulled her up close, and it made me jealous and embarrassed for him both. Nobody else seemed embarrassed though. It was like people had left their right minds at home, like the moon had stolen all their sense and put it away on the top shelf where no one could reach it.

Would they all wake up in the morning ashamed of themselves? Would they cry the way Jelly had until Seymour hugged them tight and sang at them?

When I managed to look his way again, Seymour had turned, done a half-dance in his place beside the pulpit, and was watching to the side, where one of the men keeping guard was wheeling in a big box with air holes all around the top.

I should have left right then. Should have hightailed it back to the safety of my room and the locked doors that kept the night out of our house. Instead, like a rabbit, I froze and watched that box get wheeled the rest of the way in until it was center stage. Seymour crooned at it with his wet, red mouth. He took a crowbar and loosened one side until the box panels fell away and revealed the bars of a cage. I knew what was inside before I ever saw it, some nameless instinct behind my ribs pounding out a warning—I didn't need the gasping recognition of the crowd to confirm it. That was a Reborn.

It was what I hadn't talked about with Ben and why I still had to tell Marty—a Reborn was the only thing I could think of that could have done that to the chickens. It might even have been this one, let out of its cage before the church men shut it back up and came to talk so polite to us.

Seymour threw down his crowbar, and I flinched from the solid thump of it hitting the earth at his feet. Instead of backing away from the figure in the cage—a bright-eyed Reborn crouched against the back of his cage, furthest from all those observing—Seymour moved closer to the bars. He had found himself a rhythm now, his footsteps going forward and then back and then forward again, like the dance he'd been doing earlier. The people around us all fell silent, all stopped their dancing so they could sway forward and back in time with him as he crooned to the Reborn the way I'd crooned to the chickens. Calm, calm, and calm. Soft, soft, and soft.

The Reborn focused those eyes, those terrible bright eyes, on the preacher. I held my breath, waited for an unknown awful thing to happen. The Reborn stood, moved closer to where Seymour waited by the side of his cage, right up near it like there was an electric fence between them instead of a little metal. The expected attack didn't come—the ruined man didn't lunge for Seymour. Instead, he pressed his face up tight to the bars between them.

Seymour kissed him. Full on the lips. We breathed, all we could do was breathe, but none of us spoke a word or made more than a quiet noise. It was Seymour's voice that broke the silence.

"God's holy work, God's holy messengers among us—do you believe in God, my new friends? That he'll save you from the perils of this world because you are saved in the next?" Seymour had that quiet voice out again, working the crowd, making us strain to hear him over our own blood thundering in our ears. The Reborn stood, motionless, his cheek still leaning against the bars keeping him in place. Watching Seymour. Watching us.

I wanted to get closer though I knew it was a damn fool desire. I wanted to see more of the thing's body, but no one shifted and whatever had kept me frozen before had hold of me still; I couldn't break free from it to get my legs to move. My heart got louder, so loud it was all I could hear, drowning out every other heart around me, smothering the murmurs starting up among the faithful. My eyes darted and took in what they could of the Reborn from where I was, with half the cage in shadow. Not enough, not nearly enough, and entirely too much at the same time.

Someone jostled my elbow and the sudden surprise of it was enough to break the spell of my animal response. I clutched at my arm and looked at the woman who'd knocked into me, the woman who taught the youngest children up at the school, as she walked up to Seymour—no, as she walked up past Seymour straight to the cage herself, bolder than him, with her back straight and her shoulders rigid. Once she was there, close enough the Reborn could have reached out and pulled her into his cage in little pieces like raccoons pulled chickens through wire that was too large, she relaxed. Her spine slouched and her head lolled to one side and she leaned in close to place a gentle kiss on the Reborn's cheek.

Nothing out of that one in response, though, just glittering eyes, dark as anything I'd ever seen. Less than human, not all there. More than human, maybe, and too much there. Just not right. The people around me moaned, low and impressed. Another congregation member, Elliot Franc who ran the phones in town, pushed up to be next and that finally broke me for good. I looked to where Ben had stood with Laura clutched against him, but they were both disappeared. I backed up, shaking my head, and squeezed my eyes shut as Seymour spoke again.

"It is only at the hands of those we fear, those who regard us as prey, that we learn true humility before The Lord. It is only when we put our trust in him that we are truly saved, truly spared a fate worse than death. Were I bit, were I turned, mine would be the happy end days, granted such peace by God."

Sightless, with only his voice to fill my head, my stomach churned. I had to open my eyes before I could get the gorge rising in my throat to settle. Seymour waited until Elliot had kissed the Reborn before reaching through the bars and grabbing its stiff hand like it were still made of regular flesh and blood. "Witnesses of God's power, transformed before you tonight!"

He gestured for Elliot to take the Reborn's other hand, and together they raised their arms above their heads, like a benediction.

I took flight, stumbling back to the house quick enough to set my heart pounding just as fast as it had beat in the tent. No sign of Ben, no freedom from what I'd seen. I'd laughed a little, just to myself, after my first visit in the bright of the afternoon light, but I wasn't laughing in the dark, didn't hardly have any breath for it.

Reaching the almost-safety of the house, of the old familiar back porch didn't help either. I wheezed and coughed and patted at my pockets just in case. But the truth was the truth—Ben had the key, and I was locked out on the wrong side of the door and all the walls.

I thought about banging on the door, hammering at it until Marty woke up convinced the place was burning down, until even the group up at the tent could hear me through their own ruckus. Maybe it'd make them pack up and leave, take their little pet Reborn in a box with them until they were far enough away that I didn't have to remember. Until I couldn't recall the glint of hunger in that undone man's glance when he looked at the folk what were kissing him.

The flat of my hand balled up into a fist and pulled back before I had made a conscious decision. I stopped myself, held still with my knocking hand hanging in mid-air. Waking Marty would just get us in more trouble. Chickens aside, we hadn't had any problems, and if anything were looking for anything, dinner or problems both, the lights and sounds of the congregation were probably more attractive. If I could just stay small and quiet, hide myself, I could wait until Ben came back. He had to come back.

The wood pile on the back porch probably hid more spiders than it would be smart for me to mess with. Under the porch was no better— was probably worse; there'd be more than daddy longlegs down there. No real telling what all bigger creatures might be nesting, except we didn't have sand fleas so there probably weren't any possums.

I could stay out in the open, kind of. Huddled by the door. Or I could climb in with chickens, so long as I could stand the smell.

It was something to consider, and I'd almost settled on it when that tidy pile of feathers popped into my mind again. If anything did come calling for a meal, the chicken house was the first place it would visit, and I'd be trapped, wouldn't have any other way to get out. No, that little metal building didn't hold any safety for me.

There was a storage shed, seldom used, that probably had just as many spiders as the woodpile. It was under a big old tree and further from the house than I really wanted to venture. But, like Marty said whenever we had to figure something out, danger was the mother of necessity, the grandmother of invention. I sucked up almost enough spit in my mouth to start creeping over to it when the creak of the back gate made me choke on all that moisture.

Tall, tall was all I could see in the dark. But as the form neared, I was able to swallow back my bile. "You scared the shit out of me, Ben. Where you been?"

33

My raspy whisper must not have been very intimidating. Ben gave me a smug grin when he stepped up on the back porch. I looked him over; his clothes looked rumpled and there was a dark spot on the side of his neck that looked like blood in the dark.

I'd never taken him for this stupid. "You were out necking with Laura in the dark?"

There was something more loose-limbed and easy about him than I'd ever seen before as he dug the key out of the front pocket of his jeans. "That's none of your business, Hank. And keep your voice down. You're liable to wake the whole town, carrying on like that."

Exaggeration and lies, that's what that was. But I snapped my mouth shut just the same with a click of my teeth. Ben didn't want to talk about it, that was just fine, but I'd be damned if I was going to pretend not to be mad, not after I'd been thinking about hiding in the shed. I followed him through the door, stiff-necked and high-headed, then waited for him to lock it up tight behind us.

"I'm going to bed." Where I should have been all along—I didn't say it, but it was pretty well clearly implied by the glare I gave him. Never mind that I'd been just as eager to get out there, to know what Seymour and his men did to hold back the dark. Neither of us had anticipated the way those strangers had invited the dark right into their midst, no matter how well locked up it was.

Ben nodded at me, singularly unperturbed. We'd fought too much about too many things for him to take me too seriously on this, no matter how much I wanted him to at the moment. And, to be fair— which I always hated to be—he was right. I wasn't going to hold a grudge, not over something where an equal share of the blame belonged to me.

I went to my bedroom without another word. My shirt was streaked under the arms and down the back with sour sweat, fear sweat. It clung to my back as I stripped and wadded it up with my other discarded clothes at the foot of the bed. I'd pick them up in the morning or catch hell with Marty for being messy. My skin felt cold enough for me to fumble for my flannel pajamas, the ones folded up at the back of my closet. They were soft. Turning on a light was too much like inviting trouble; I'd seen enough already for the night so I felt around for a pair of clean socks. Once my feet were settled, there was nothing else to distract me or keep from me climbing under my sheets.

Even after I'd run my hands all over my body, made sure every part was right where it belonged, it took a long time to fall asleep.

In the morning, my dreams hovered in my peripheral vision but refused to come into focus. I kept quiet, determined to keep my tongue behind my teeth. If I started to tell Marty about the chickens, the whole story would come tumbling out. Including how much I'd wanted to go up and kiss that Reborn myself.

I did my chores by rote. And when Ben headed out in the truck, I tagged along, in the back so the rush of the engine would drown out my desire to touch that of which I should be afraid.

CHAPTER FOUR

Pressure Front

Y'all come in," Marty called to us. **"It's fixing to storm." She** stood on the back porch, a sculpture of dark wrinkled parchment wrapped in a big white apron and fighting the wind to keep the fabric from flying up. Marty believed in decorum.

It'd been two weeks since we snuck out. I'd worked myself to a tired nub just to avoid looking out at that forsaken tent. And now it was finally gone. They'd been packing up early while I fed the chickens. Every tidy bundle they'd loaded onto a truck had made it easier to stand up straight. And when they'd wheeled that box to the back of Seymour's truck, a shiver of relief tickled me all the way to my heels.

"It's always fixing to storm." Ben let the old truck run for a minute. Then he cranked his window closed, switched her off, and climbed out. He banged the side of the bed with the flat of his tanned hand. "Come on. You know she'll stand there until we come inside."

The sun—and the giddy relief of Seymour's absence—had made us both lazy. Ben had been short-tempered, but now he smiled at me.

The noise made me jump even though I'd been watching him. Ben was right—Marty was stubborn and if she wanted us both inside, that's where we'd be. I swung my leg over the tailgates, found the bumper with my dirty bare foot, and hopped over and down to the deep-piled pine straw that cushioned the back drive.

The sky was hanging low—heavier than my guilt every one of these past mornings. Now that the revival tent was gone, I had wanted to go over to Jenny's place, but there didn't seem like any way Marty was going to let me out. No matter what Ben said, Marty had a knack with the weather—and the few stolen kisses we'd managed recently in the back of Jenny's daddy's barn weren't worth getting caught in a bad storm, even if I'd been willing to sneak out again after my last experience. Things didn't look to be shaping up for another empty lightning storm.

I trudged behind Ben with my eyes on my feet, through the knee-high grass next to the rough steps up onto the back porch, thinking more about Jenny's breasts and the way her tiny waist felt pressed against my rounded belly than I was about anything else. Marty ushered us through the backdoor and then locked up behind us. That's when I stopped staring at my toes.

There was a stranger at the kitchen table.

Not even a stranger—I had seen him before. Wearing that suit when everyone else was limp from the heat and damp with sweat under the tent. He'd watched Jelly and Seymour just like I had and hadn't been moved a jot by any of it.

"Ben, Hank," Marty introduced us. "This is your cousin James." She had wrapped her apron around her tiny hands, a nervous gesture I'd only witnessed a few times; the last had been as she waited to see if our old dog would survive the night. Daisy hadn't, and Marty had buried her upside down just in case. "Say hello now." She turned away from us, went to the sink, and started in on the lunch dishes.

The stranger—James—didn't stand. He just looked us over.

"Hello." Ben managed to be a friendly sort for the most part when he wasn't feeling protective. He reached out, offered his hand to shake. Cousin James let Ben's hand hang in the air for a moment before he reached out to take it. I could tell he didn't like the dirt under Ben's nails, didn't like the dust ground into the skin of his palm.

James's hand, when he extended it, was pale and soft, like he'd never done any outside work.

37

"You must be Benjamin." He had a smooth voice, even paler than his palms, that burned on the way down, like the cold whiskey Big Wayne had let us sip when we delivered his papers. He took out a pocket handkerchief and wiped both hands, then folded the square and tucked it away again. "You're taller than I expected. How old are you now?"

He hadn't said a word to me, barely looked at me, but I didn't fool myself. He knew I was there—and would get to me when he had business with me. He made me sweat, slick in my armpits that was going to stink like being scared, so I wasn't in a hurry for that business to come up.

"It's just Ben, sir, and I'm eighteen." Ben's shoulders were thrown back. He was lying—he wouldn't be eighteen for another month, but it was close enough. Ben had shot up a foot and a half over the past year, so he was taller than half of the town men, even though he was skinny. He stood still when James got up, walked around him to take a gander at Ben's long legs and bony chest, to look with a little sneer at the messy thatch of Ben's brown hair going every which direction. He'd been driving with the windows down.

James reached into his pocket again, but this time he pulled out a little notebook. He flipped it open and looked at Marty, like he was asking a question. When she nodded, he picked up the phone receiver on the wall, waited for the operator. Marty must have hooked the phone up just for him—we were wired for it, but hardly ever used it so the thing generally stayed shut up in a cabinet.

He gave Harriet—it had to be Harriet working today—a number he read from his little book and then it was silent while we all waited for someone to answer him.

"I've found him." He paused to listen. "Yes, he's still seventeen."

He hadn't bought that lie then.

There was a longer pause this time, and James frowned, an expression that made his forehead ugly. It smoothed out though, before he spoke again, "See you then."

He settled the phone back into its cradle and turned back to Ben with his hand still on the receiver like he was holding on to something.

"You need to go and pack a bag. Don't bother bringing anything other than clothes." James turned his back, sat down at the table again. There were papers, not handwritten, spread in front of him, and he studied those like they were important. We might as well have not even been there for all the attention he spared us.

None of it made any sense. Ben stood there, his mouth open like a fly trap, and then he turned to Marty. "What's going on?" He was taller than her by a good measure, but in that moment he looked like a little kid, his face wide open with confusion—all of his practice at hiding his feelings didn't make any difference when it came to this.

She didn't even turn around and that scared me more than anything else ever had. Her washing the dishes was ordinary and everyday—and the way she wasn't stopping made my eyes water. She'd never shied away from bad news, had never been afraid to tell us when bad things happened. Marty had been the one to tell us when our parents and her husband had died, were all killed by a drunk when I was five, and then buried out on the side of the road without any markers to keep track of them. But Marty just stayed steady on washing dishes that were already clean like she was trying to wear the shine off of them.

Her voice was clear at least. "Go do what he tells you, Ben. He'll explain it all later." The plate in her hands slipped, broke with a crack against the bottom of the sink, and her head dropped forward. "Henrietta, go with your brother."

She never used my full name like that, hadn't since we came to live with her year round. It was Marty that had started calling me Hank in the first place. Ben and I looked at each other—we knew when we were being dismissed even if we didn't much like it—and he jerked his head toward the back of the house. He moved slow, but I didn't wait for him. I was out of the kitchen and halfway down the hall to his room before I thought about my feet walking.

Of course, Ben was going to do what Marty told him to do. We always did, had since we'd first come to stay with her. But just as much as any of that, I could tell a real simple thing: he thought James was weird, but the man wasn't making Ben's skin crawl. Not the way mine was threatening to itch right off my body. Worse yet, for the life of me—or him—I couldn't string together any words that could talk Ben out of going along with it, either, not once he started folding his jeans.

By the time he was finished packing, Ben's bag bulged, stuffed with shirts and pants and socks and clean underwear, ragged but wearable like most of our clothes. There was also a book and a pocketknife because Ben was going to do just what James instructed—but I wasn't. And Ben wasn't going to work too hard to stop me. Which was smart.

Marty served an early supper like James was some kind of welcome house guest, but we all picked at it. And after, Ben stood beside his bag on the front porch, the late afternoon cutting through the promise of a storm and making it a lie. Ben hugged me tight. Marty stayed in the kitchen, gone back to washing dishes again.

The shiny dark blue car in the driveway—where Seymour's truck had been the last thing to park—had pulled up halfway through the meal. James—and I had my doubts about him being any kind of cousin after all that time spent in silence and the way he'd left most of his food uneaten on his plate—was already in the front passenger seat, looking impatient.

The car's horn had split the silence, no family conversation, not even a recounting of the fine morning we'd spent carrying papers around and delivering them to houses that were closer to the woods even if they weren't so far out as we were from town. We backed up to scrub and low bushes. James had put down his fork when the horn sounded, stood up, and motioned for Ben to follow.

That was when Marty had headed back to the sink. She'd refused to come out, and I had been left alone to trail after my brother and James—who had still barely even acknowledged my existence, had barely seemed to see me even as he gave the sense he knew everything about me, right down to my promise not to tell Jenny's boyfriend about how she'd let me put my hand up her skirt.

Ben hugged me tight, and I let him. We weren't real affectionate on a daily basis, but this weren't much of a normal day.

"I don't know what this is all about, but I'll call as soon as I can— keep the phone set up." Ben's whisper in my ear was comforting even though I could hear his heart racing, feel his pulse pounding. "In the meantime, take care of yourself and Marty for me."

That was a strange notion—Marty had always taken care of us, not the other way around. When I struggled to remember our parents, I could still remember Marty, and it had all been okay.

Nothing else made sense to do though so I promised. "I will. You take care of yourself." I hugged him back again, hard, then pulled away. I was sixteen. Too old to hang on to him like I was a baby, even though everything about him leaving felt wrong.

He paused, hand still on my shoulder, looked at the car. James didn't honk again or shout out the window. But his stare hadn't let up since Ben had stayed with me on the porch to say goodbye. "Be safe. Just be safe." It was that grown-up voice, and it hurt me like sand in my eyes.

I nodded, tongue between my molars to distract me so I wouldn't bust out crying. I watched his back when he turned and walked away, down the steps and over to the car, where he climbed in the backseat. He held himself like he thought a man should, like he'd practiced when we were little, imitating the men on television when we'd been able to pick up a signal, before the channel had faded and Marty had put a tablecloth over the big box with the screen. I straightened my own shoulders, a good foot shorter than him and all plump to his lanky, hazel eyes to his green, mess to his good intentions.

If it were the last time I ever saw him—because something felt terrible, like it just might be—I wanted him to see me strong.

The car drove off, a dust plume visible behind it even when I couldn't pick the car itself out anymore.

Marty wasn't in the kitchen when I finally went back inside. The water still ran in the sink though, the faucet cranked at a funny angle so the water pooled on the counter, spilled over the edges, and splashed onto the floor. I jogged over to twist the tap and shut it off, then stood for a moment to look out the window.

It didn't have a real good angle on the porch, but the end of the driveway, where you'd have to turn either right or left, was in clear view. That was how she'd watched Ben leave.

A crash sounded from the back of the house, and I almost jumped out of my skin. My foot slipped in the puddle on the floor, and I flailed, banged my wrist on the counter so it hurt when I caught myself. I was never exactly graceful—I managed okay most times, but was used to catching myself right before a fall. The noise boomed again, and I lost my grip, tried to scramble, and almost fell instead, then turned it into a hitching run, headed toward the source of the racket.

Marty's room. Ben and I had the two tiny rooms at the front of the house. They'd been ours since we'd been grown enough to be left alone all night long—Ben since we moved in and me not too long after that. For all I'd lived here more than ten years now, I'd only been in Marty's bedroom a handful of times. I hesitated at her door, hand on the polished wood frame.

I couldn't just barge in—a lifetime of manners wouldn't let me step over the saddle. Manners, Marty always said, were just about the only thing we had left to keep us civilized. "Marty? Are you in here?"

Manners didn't keep me from using my eyes though. The big oak dresser, with its mirror framed in carved oak leaves, was a wreck. The drawers were pulled out, hanging open, and the mirror itself lay shattered on the floor. That must have been the first crash. There was a full-length mirror, too, twisted in its stand and broken in the corner. That must have been the second.

And Marty was on the floor between the two, on her knees, apron pulled up over her face to muffle her sobs.

I forgot my manners entirely, rushing right in without invitation. Marty never cried. The broken glass had scattered everywhere, and the floorboards creaked when I hit my knees so hard down beside her.

"Hank, you go to your room." Her eyes were red, already swollen from tears like a creek overflowing its bed. Her voice was harsh, quiet without being a whisper, hoarse instead of steady. I ignored her, all my obedience used up on letting Ben leave, and she shook her head at me. "Hank, listen to me now." She was trying to sound stronger, but I shook my head right back at her.

"Who was that man?" Ben had told me to take care of her, this crumpled up woman who had never done more than bend a little in a flood. "Ben's gone now—what's going on?" I sounded grown up even to my own ears, like Ben had left me something of his voice, deeper toned and more serious than I'd been before James—before Seymour—had come to visit.

"Watch out for the glass." Instead of answering, Marty hugged me, smoothed back the long tangle of my hair. The ride in the pickup bed had knotted it up and flung it everywhere.

My hair was the only thing I ever felt vain about, even though Laura made fun of me for not having it brushed all the time. It would have been more practical to cut it short, but my mother wore hers long, one of my only clear memories of her. It felt right to keep mine long, too.

The weight of it hung heavy down my back and tangles snagged in Marty's fingers. I promised myself I'd take extra care with the brush before bed so she'd be able to touch it from now on, like I was bargaining with the future in the hopes things would go back to some kind of normal.

I curled my toes, kept my feet under me as I rocked there in her embrace. There were sure to be slivers on both of us, but they would wait. "Who was he?" That seemed to be the most important question. If there was just an answer to that, there'd be answers to everything else.

There was no way to be prepared for the answer.

"He's your cousin, right enough—your daddy's oldest brother's boy. Teddy stayed in the city, took up with a divorced woman there and never bothered to send James out to us." Something fierce sparked in her eyes, and I knew there had been some scenes about that. Marty took living out here seriously and had her opinions about folks that never left town, much less the big city.

Then she closed her eyes, and the thin lids quivered with whatever she remembered.

When we had first moved in with Marty, Ben and I had been afraid of just about everything. Our parents hadn't left the city all that often themselves, and they'd filled us up with nightmares about the things that bumped around in the country night. We hadn't been able to sleep without a light on. Marty had sat in a chair between our beds—we'd shared a room those first few weeks—and told us stories without lights on until we'd been okay with the dark inside the house.

Marty had started every story by closing her eyes and breathing in a great lungful of air until we thought she'd pop. She inhaled like that now, her ribs creaking with it as she found her voice again.

CHAPTER FIVE

There's A Story She Could Tell

Years ago, it's been fifty years now, when the Reborn first rose, people still thought things were going to go back to normal. That they'd wake up one day and the dust storms would be over, and the plumbing would start up again, and the television would broadcast more than silent movies from old Hollywood.

Of course, when things didn't, when we all woke up covered in fine sand and had to draw water from the well, and even the radio wasn't reliable, people got angry. They stayed angry for a long time, too—madder about the war than they had ever been when we were fighting it. When my daddy locked up the doors at night, he wasn't worried about the Reborn coming for us— they were too far off, a rumor of a nightmare. They only came in with the fresh dust at first, and all we got was stale, blown clear across the country.

No, he locked the door against women and men who figured if they couldn't beg something or borrow it, then they'd steal it. After Louis Masterson down the road got his head stove in with his own shovel by a couple of drifters after his bacon, Daddy reinforced the doors and showed us all the secret spots he'd added in our closets to hide in, just in case.

Life hadn't changed all that much for us. We were plum happy about the biggest difference—we didn't have to ride the city bus to typing school anymore so we could hope to earn ourselves jobs before we found ourselves husbands, no more two hours to the next town over in the mornings before the sun came up. But we still did all our usual chores and went dancing at night and didn't really think about what was driving all those people crazy in the first place.

After all, it wasn't our problem. I was only twenty-two. And my little sister Cassie and me, we didn't care about the drought out west; we cared about Lyle Hendricks's new car, and Mazzie Way's new dress, and how we could ride in one and copy the other. At most, we wondered if it was ever going to rain here again or if the farmers out there had ruined it for everyone.

Oh, the clouds would gather. The clouds would gather, and the winds would pick up, whipping our clothes tight on our bodies as we ran for cover so we could stay out of the wet. But the wet never actually came. It'd either stay just as bone dry as a funeral for a miser, the air full of mean electricity, or we'd get sand instead of rain, pouring through cracks in the door, silt blown in from the Midwest, from California if the gossip was to be believed.

Belief is a powerful thing, Hank. It'll make things happen that ought not, just because the mind's stronger than the real world. What chance does reality have when people are so cussed stubborn about the things they think they see?

Or maybe they really did see bogeymen, coming out of those storms. Maybe they really did see the faces, worn from their time in the ground, of their loved ones coming back hungry and cold and bitter. I was naïve, and I didn't know then that life could be so hard. Maybe I shouldn't be one to doubt.

Travelers—refugees, really—told us the stories in bits and drabs like dirty dish water dripping from a rag.

The dead, they came out of the boxes they'd been laid in. It started in the Dakotas, frozen ground refusing our human remains like we'd offended the earth itself. People thought it was the apocalypse—maybe it was. Maybe that's what all this is, and there's just no god around to sort us all out one from another after all.

Some people met the walkers with open arms—longed-for husbands and brothers and daughters and wives. They were the first to find out that the dead are hungry. They need to feed whatever's giving them a second kind of life, another turn around the sun, a chance to be Reborn.

We kept to ourselves at first, all huddled around Daddy, and Daddy *huddled close up to the radio, trying to tune in, to catch some explanation for it. Those days we mostly heard about the new war, the new war brewing up overseas. But then, the scientists started up about how we stripped the land of grass and everybody else started up about how we stripped the land of magic until there was nothing for it to do but pick up and leave, look for a new home all the way at the ocean, dust on the railings of ships bound for England or France or Cuba. Back then, in the middle of it, half the neighbors still just figured we'd all been cursed. Might have even deserved it, too, grabbing land the way folks did.*

It took a while for the stories to spread, even with the radio reports. And just behind the stories moved the Reborn. Walking—running—all over the country, visiting loved ones and gnawing them to the quick until all the love ran right out. People tried to fight, tried to put their own back into the ground. But the Reborn are fast, and they're strong, and there's something in their eyes. They're too canny to be easy to put down; they don't want to go back now that they walk again.

Can't say as I blame them for that, not entirely. But they ain't who they used to be, no matter who they used to be. Can anyone be once they've crossed over and then stood back up?

The government tried. Upped the bulletins until we all turned our radios off because there wasn't ever any good news or music anymore. We stayed in the loop about how the scientists were working on a cure, passing news around like a collection plate at church. All the other news fell behind; we didn't even hear much about the new war for a long time, being fought in Europe. The war stayed away from us, too, no one over there wanting to bring our troubles home to their battlefields. Didn't do them any good in the end. Their dead rose, from stinking trenches and muck-covered fields that were carpeted with dying folks. Dying folks who just served as food.

Eventually, though I don't know how long it took for the news to reach us, the war ended. With a whimper, not a bang. I reckon people in Europe and even over in Asia are still trying to recover from it, all those Reborn wandering around trying to find the homes they were fighting for in the first place.

One of the things you've got to understand is that they've always been working on a cure. The more it spread, the more people got involved in looking. Hell or high water, someone in some laboratory has always been working on setting the world back to the way it was, back to the way people think it ought to be. Man wasn't meant to live more than one life, that's what we were all told.

Not everyone believed that though. There were a few—not many but a couple like that Seymour and his ilk—who thought the Reborn were holy. Touched by God. Chosen for a second chance at life on earth. Thing was, the way they were behaving with dragging folks screaming into the street for feeding on, it wasn't a real popular idea to try to get across. But you can't stop the faithful. Or the greedy. Missionaries preached it, even knocked on our door with their fool ideas before Daddy turned them away with a shotgun pointed at their heads.

People needed something to believe. They always do.

Religion, Hank, will trump science just about every goddamn time.

Life finally changed in ways we noticed. No more new cars and no more new dresses, and me and Cassie did worry about that because, so we'd been promised, things were supposed to get better after the war. We'd have better things as a great nation. What we got instead was those who walk and those who eat.

And it kept getting worse instead of better. More of the Reborn, spreading further and faster. The preachers kept pace, dogging the heels of the hungry as they blew east with the wind. More and more died, starving and choking on all that dirt in the air. The dead were laid down one day and then some of them were up three days later, gnawing at the doors barred against them.

It took a handful of years to make it all the way here; Florida sunshine calling them to come on down with the rest of the tourists even in death. We didn't get many storms—we'd always had sand, and it took a lot to get it to blow. But the clouds clashed above us, and the wind kicked up a ruckus at night, worse than it ever had and howling across the tin roof. It was a long, dry stretch for folks to walk all the way out here.

We started sinking our dead off the coast when they didn't get burned or buried face down so they'd dig themselves deeper instead of breaking out of their graves—that meant we didn't see many of our own close kin, just the long-lost brothers who'd gone out west to seek fortunes, the runaway wives who wandered back to their left-behind husbands and children, prodigal sons and daughters looking for lambs.

By the time they crossed the state line in any real number, the government had been working on a solution long enough to have ideas to try. Lyle—he kept running that car of his even when most other folks took to riding horses again, and that's how he persuaded me to give him a try—came home with some papers from the government one day, recruiting him to do some work for them, studying the Reborn in the area, tracking their movements and behavior. He took to it, like a man born to science and general nosiness. He kept an eye on how the things did their business and reported back.

Those government folks got my daddy involved, too. He and Lyle would go out scouting and come back filthy and happy with a day's worth of work, information all written down in tiny notebooks until they started staying out for a whole week at a time. It wasn't bad. It wasn't the way things had been, but I thought it was good. Maybe even better because we weren't at war anymore, we were taking care of things at home and seeing to our own troubles.

Cassie took up with Lyle's little brother. And then, before I knew it, they were working with the government boys, too. It might not actually have been the real government at that point. Everything started to get real secret. Classified, they called it. Not a one of them was forthcoming about who was keeping us paid in gasoline and milk and sugar and other staple goods. But it was too good just to have a job, too good to pass up, and Lyle got more of the family swept up in it.

I was so proud of him. He took good care of me, Hank, good care of all of us. I wouldn't have traded him for anyone else.

But good times never last. We should have learned that if we didn't learn anything else. The Reborn stayed the same, but people got meaner, kept more to themselves. The cities got their luxuries back, most of them, and everyone there just wanted to forget, as much as they could, as much as the Reborn would allow. But you can't forget when you live out this far from anyone. It wasn't just drifters anymore, it was your own neighbor you had to watch out for. It took a long time to trust folks, but we thought we had time. We always thought we had time.

CHAPTER SIX

Bad Luck Ain't No Luck

T hings are speeding up now," Marty's voice was a rasp, long past the need for a drink of water. "And I can't keep track of them all anymore. James works for those same government folks, the ones Lyle and your parents worked for. Trying to find a cure. But time keeps running out."

It sounded like they'd all been working together so long that even the ones who weren't family really were family after all. It sounded creepy.

I knew most of this though, sort of. Hell, almost everyone knew how the Reborn had come crawling out of the woods and into our houses like people's homes were larders to be opened up and eaten clean. But I hadn't known about James, hadn't known about my parents working for the government. Marty grasped my left hand, turned my palm up on her own, and traced down wide around the mound of my thumb with her thumbnail.

"You see this line? It's your lifeline. Used to, people would tell you your fortune just by looking at your palm. Ain't any line for being Reborn though, no line on any palm for that." She finally met my gaze, eyes ablaze with something, with anger like I'd never seen from her before. "Only thing the government ever figured out was how to make someone rise again on purpose."

I knew that, too. And I knew, in my gut, what she wasn't saying— whether out of loyalty to family or because she wasn't sure. James was going to turn Ben, my brother, my family, in pursuit of something. They were going to starve Ben for as long as they could, as long as he could stay alive until he was right up on the edge of dying; they'd give him no food until he was so hungry he'd see things out of the corners of his eyes, things that shouldn't be there because Ben had the Sight, just like I did, even though he never talked about Seeing anything, hadn't talked about it since we were real little. When he finally fell, pushed over by one of the things that only existed where he could See them, James—or someone he worked with, someone with soft hands like his—would offer Ben tainted meat, the meat of a Reborn who didn't need their flesh anymore, who walked around mostly bones and hollow echoes of sounds that no one would survive hearing.

Marty wasn't saying anything more, but she didn't have to because maybe no one knew all the details about how the first Reborn rose—other than the dust—but everyone knew how more Reborn were made: you starved off the mortal flesh, and then they ate the offering, skin and all. The person who was changing slept. They slept, and they woke up touched, sacred and profane in someone like Seymour's eyes all at once, and it was the job of all the rest of us to keep safe out of the way while that person fed. While they found their first prey.

It was supposedly holy—a sacred process, according to the folks who liked to jaw about it. I hadn't heard it over in that big tent, but unspoken didn't mean a damn thing when everyone believed. We'd talked about it when I was little, down by the river as we played and fished—and played when we were supposed to be fishing. My friends knew it, sure as I knew Marty didn't take us to church on Sundays, didn't really seem to have any care for the godly words that were supposed to keep us safe. I guessed now that she'd known too much to have any faith left over.

That was why we had more chickens than we needed for our meat and eggs. And the goats. Just in case someone showed up hungry. We hadn't always been so prepared—Daisy's hind end had been chewed to the bone, her soft muzzle untouched by the gaunt man who'd shambled off when he'd had his fill of muscle torn off her haunches. We'd never gotten another dog. None of us had enough heart left in us for that. But we had plenty of birds. And the occasional pile of feathers.

I rose up, pulled my hand out of hers. Felt the prick of glass in my heel as I backed out of Marty's room, away from what she had already said and what she had implied. I turned and ran back down the hall to my own room, but it wasn't safe, nowhere was safe anymore. I crossed my own bloody footprints in the hall and headed for the back porch.

Marty barred my way. I hadn't even heard her moving. "They'll come for you in two years. They just keep taking people, and there won't be anyone left to take once they take you—there's no more in our family line. They say it's for their cure—but I don't reckon there is one, not anymore if there ever was to begin with."

"Why'd you let James take Ben?" I couldn't leave—and I had to leave—without knowing that. "If you knew, why'd you let them?" There was no way I could stay in Marty's house, not with them coming for me and not with the way she'd just stood there with her back to us while James looked Ben up and down and decided he'd do right fine for their experiments. Marty had taken care of us, protected us; she'd loved us and we'd loved her right back—and then she'd given Ben over to them without even a fight. It wasn't fair that love couldn't keep us out of her mess.

"There's no way to stop them. There's no way to believe what people keep believing in, and people believe in the Reborn the way they believe in a curse from God." Marty herded me back toward the kitchen and her face was stone. "But they don't get to have you, they don't get to take you, too, not if I help."

Was she really going to help? I couldn't read anything in her face anymore. And she'd let them take my brother without any sort of fight. She'd just given him up.

"Let me help you, Hank. I'll pack you some food and tell you something else you need to know." She had me there. She knew I was made of curious.

If there was a chance to save Ben, if I could act fast and make some sort of difference for him, I'd do it. The car had turned right at the end of the drive, heading toward the city at speeds I couldn't match on my own two feet. No way to catch up, no way to even know where to look to find them. Marty's information was the only thing that might make a difference. And I had always trusted her, even though it seemed like I had trusted her all these years to no good end.

I stepped toward the kitchen, and the pain in my heel finally caught up with me, finally registered. I bit my lip with every step to keep from crying out. Ben wouldn't have cried, so I wouldn't let myself either. It seemed important, like some small connection to him. Marty must have seen me flinch anyway because she pulled out a chair and fussed until I sat, the release from hurt as good as breaking the surface of the pond for air when we were out swimming.

She bustled over to the pantry. "Stay right there a minute and let me get the first aid box." Her back, stooped over ever since I found her on her bedroom floor, straightened up again with purpose. At least, for a little while.

What was going to happen to Marty once I was gone? Sure, she'd do fine surviving on her own, she was strong even if she was always talking about being old, but was she going to be lonely? That thought, raw and new, hurt the same way my steps to the chair had, each one grinding that shard of glass deeper into the meat of my foot.

I couldn't walk to the city like that—though it was a better feeling than the glass cutting right through my heart. "Where are they?" That was all I needed to know.

Marty knelt on stiff joints, tweezers and bandages in hand, the second time I'd seen her on the floor in the space of ten minutes. She shook her head at me and went to work with the tweezers. There was more glass than I'd realized—if I'd set out to walk on it, I'd have caught an infection in no time. It still felt wrong for her to be taking such care of me, and not just because of today with James. A certain feeling that I was never going to see her again made my throat seize up like I'd eaten something, to which I was powerfully allergic. I didn't want Marty alone. Didn't want her to die either, that was for damn sure.

And it could happen. She'd been on her own before we'd come along, but she'd gotten used to us, she told us that all the time, too. Who was going to chop the stove wood with Ben done and gone? Who was going to mind those stupid chickens with me out on my own?

She'd said I had two years—I could wait. Hell, I didn't have to go with James when he came back neither, assuming he did. It might not even be him when it happened, and Marty wouldn't let a real stranger into the house no matter who they claimed they worked for or what they wanted.

Marty started on my other foot, wiping the dirt and blood away with a kitchen towel. The fabric caught on a sliver in my sole, snagged it and pulled it, and sent a quick slice of pain up my nerves. "You can't go after him, Hank. You have to accept that Ben is gone and there's nothing you can do." She focused her gaze on the tweezers, the same pair that had removed countless splinters from our fingers before she'd kissed our foreheads and sent us back out to play.

"That's not good enough." That was never going to be good enough. Where was the Marty who'd encouraged us, told us that as long as we got our chores done first, we could do anything?

"It has to be. You're a child still and have to know your limits. Learning that is part of growing up, and right now it's time to grow up." Her work on my feet turned quick and efficient. She ran the kitchen towel over both of them again, then smeared my soles with ointment. "Here, put these on." She handed me a clean pair of white socks, her shattered reflections all cleaned out of my flesh.

"So, I'm supposed to just let them turn him without any kind of trying to put a stop to it?" I pulled the socks on, obedient in that even as I protested. I'd been lucky to avoid any major cuts, and the socks felt good and snug. "I'm supposed to just sit back and let them test cures that won't work until I don't even know what happens?"

This wasn't a curse from god—Marty had seen to it herself that we'd known better even though she'd never told us the whole story. Was she telling me the whole story even now? But sure as anything, they weren't going to find a cure by locking Ben up in a lab, maybe in a cage like the one I'd seen under the tent, leaving him hungry all the time while they tested things on him that didn't work. It wouldn't be him anymore, no matter what else.

Marty shook her towel at me. "That's exactly what you're supposed to do. Because if you don't, they'll take you and do the same thing to you." Her eyes looked wet, like she was already mourning me and Ben. "I thought I could find a way to stop them, tried to tell them he weren't going to be useful to them, that he didn't have the Sight and neither do you. But they didn't believe me, and here we are. You need to look out for yourself now. You just go on, Hank, and let the world do its worst."

The moisture in her eyes that she wasn't letting fall magnified her until she was swimming—I blinked fast and heavy, and she cleared up again. It was my own eyes that were wet—hers were dry as a bone. No matter how they'd threatened her, she wasn't crying over it now.

I wanted it to be early morning again: sunlight coming in through the curtains and my idle speculation about Jenny's ankles slipping away gentle and smooth while I blinked sleep, not tears, from my eyes. Morning, with Ben out back starting up the truck and me grabbing bits of sausage direct from the hot pan, juggling them from palm to palm so the grease didn't burn my fingers while Marty hollered at me to find a plate and eat like a civilized human being instead of a damn Reborn.

Instead, it had turned full dark while we were in her room. Night had struck early and swift while we weren't paying attention, and Jenny's fine legs were further from my hands than they'd ever been. I'd never see her again either. Nor Laura, Jelly, or anyone else under that tent. Pitch dark of night outside, when all the doors were meant to stay locked and everyone found an inside to stay in so they'd be safe from predators they couldn't even see coming.

My feet looked strange in the clean white socks Marty had given me—her own socks, not one of my dingy pairs full of holes. I stood and looked down at where Marty still crouched, the only way I'd ever be taller than her. She had never led us wrong in anything else. And I knew she was right no matter how a yell was still trapped in my throat to accuse her of lying. I didn't have what I needed to follow that car and walk out of wherever it was going with Ben in tow and in the same shape he'd been in when he left. Ben was smart, smarter than me— though he always argued the same thing in reverse. I had to trust him to look after his own self and all but heard his voice saying the same thing, telling me to take care of myself instead of throwing in with his troubles all catawampus.

"Where am I supposed to go?" I sounded steady. Marty had never failed to give an honest answer to a direct question. I wasn't going to say it was just bad luck I'd never asked her directly about men coming to take us away for experiments, but she wouldn't change her ways entirely. I didn't think. And I needed her answer.

"I don't know. I don't know where you're going to wind up, Hank, anymore than I knew where your parents and my man were going to." Marty's smile was soft and a little broken around the edges. "Just stay away from the city. That's where they'll start looking for you when they realize you aren't here."

I didn't know what to do with that, didn't know what she meant when she'd always told us the same story about a drunk driver. They weren't going anywhere, not as far as I knew. There were questions to ask, but there wasn't time to ask them, not the way Marty was rushing me.

According to her, I had two years before they came for me. But it made sense they'd keep an eye on the place. When I disappeared, would they show up and offer to find me? Would she tell them I ran off, just a wild girl upset over losing her brother, and she was sure I'd turn up? She might tell my friends that—but with that red baseball cap in the middle of our field, could she manage the lie with a straight face?

Marty creaked back on her heels, looking up at me. "Stick to the back trails. I know you have most of those old woods mapped out in your head like the back of your hand. Keep safe in there and stay on the move south, away from them. Don't let anyone catch you unawares."

It bothered me, Marty on the floor like that, almost more than her warning made me uneasy. I reached down to help her up. Ben had told me to take care of her. I laughed, kind of sick in my stomach and newly bitter at the thought of it. I was going to fail at the only thing he'd asked of me. My laugh sounded strange to my ears as Marty straightened up until we were looking at each other eye to eye.

She'd always been tall and straight and proud, but now she was bent and small, right at my level. It would have been better to blame it on me not noticing my own growth into my heavy bones, but the truth was that it had happened in her bedroom before I'd followed her in there; it had happened when she broke her mirrors and tossed her drawers around. In those violent moments, the years had come down on Marty and outnumbered all of the ones she'd lived.

"So I'm just supposed to survive?" That didn't seem like much. I knew where to find food and could probably figure out shelter if I bent my mind to it. I could cover my own tracks. Surely there was more to do, more to my running away than that. "What else should I do?"

"That ain't a half bad goal on its own, girl. You stick to it, it'll be enough." Marty patted my arm, headed over to the pantry. Marty couldn't ever send anyone off without food, for all most of Ben's last meal had gone uneaten.

I had vague memories of sitting tiny next to a basket done up in red and white, food for the drive back to wherever we were driving back to. I couldn't remember and Ben was gone so he couldn't remember it for me. I wasn't going to have the time to ask Marty, things moving too fast to find my answers now. Despite my earlier bravado, the supplies from her would help. But I was leaving so much, things I'd never get to learn.

The bag Marty brought me, packed while I was lost in my thoughts, was heavy with food so at least I wasn't going to go hungry for a while. She had worked quickly, and I'd just stood there like a child. Lost. And I couldn't afford to be that at this point.

"Go get your boots. And pack a small bag—light but smart. Take what you can because you won't be coming back." Marty whispered that last part, put into words what I'd been feeling since the afternoon had spun out of ordinary control. She wouldn't look me in the eyes anymore, already saying goodbye to me, already willing me out of her head so she could carry on.

She'd taught us that, after all—what was reality if people believed something else hard enough? She stood there, right in front of me, believing me out of existence until I was gone. My eyes blurred again but I wiped them with the hand that wasn't twisted in the neck of my food sack. Crying just wasted water, Marty had always said. She hadn't been wrong about that. And now it was like she had already forgotten Ben, like he was long lost instead of barely out of the driveway. It wouldn't take her much longer to forget me.

I left her in the kitchen; she wasn't going to follow me. I headed to my room—my only room, my last room. I wasn't packing Ben's bag this time but my own. I'd collected little things over the years: tiny dolls Marty had told me were over a hundred years old, shells from the one time we'd gone to the beach though it had been three hours to the coast in the back of the truck, bouncing over potholes and through security blockades. I even had a few books. Some fairytales, a novel that my mother had left behind before she was killed. I had already known the basics of reading before we moved in with Marty and she'd always encouraged me to practice.

The books got left on the shelf. They'd get too heavy after a while, heavier than I'd want to carry for long distances. And they'd get ruined in the eventual rain unless I found a dry place to hole up. No matter how much I loved the stories, there was no sense to it—and I had them in my head anyway.

I packed socks, underwear, the bras I had to wear even though I hated them. An extra pair of jeans and two long-sleeved t-shirts because it was better to be too hot than too cold and there were ticks in the woods. You couldn't just wish for new clothes when you were freezing or picking bugs out of your armpits. I sat long enough to lace up my boots.

I turned to leave, but remembered before I crossed the threshold. We didn't really need hidey-holes, but I'd had one just for the thrill of it. It felt childish now, but I'd been a child as recently as the day before. Tucking myself into the back of my closet, I fished out the box from the little compartment that Marty didn't know I knew about. Just a small wooden cigar box—probably already old as dirt when I'd claimed it for mine, the smell of tobacco long aired out. It was for my treasures. There weren't many. A few pretty rocks, a piece of green bottle glass smooth on all its edges, and my mother's wedding ring. I didn't know where my father's was—maybe Ben had hidden it in his treasure spot, but there was no way to find it now if he hadn't managed to pack it when I wasn't looking. The ring just about fit, was only a little big on my ring finger. I tried it on the middle finger of my right hand, which was better. I didn't want to be careless and lose it.

Habit dictated that I put my box back where I always hid it. Maybe one day Marty would find it, cleaning out my room for some reason or another. For whatever came next for her. I picked my food sack back up and slung my backpack over my shoulder. I left my room, the hallway, the kitchen. All of it.

The storm Marty had warned us about was blowing all around the house now, dust and a little bit of rain both flying around until I tasted dirt in my mouth without even opening the door. The wind pulled at the door when I opened it and then pushed at it when I tried to close it behind me. And then I stood on the wrong side of the locked door, Marty looking at me through the little bit of glass. I could break it, raise my fist and batter it into pieces and maybe not be any worse off than my feet already were. It was tempting, and for one, two, three heartbeats, it was all I could imagine, all I could see happening. I'd break that glass and reach through to unlock the door and Marty would follow me back into the kitchen and make me a plate full of leftover food. We'd cry together, later that night, about Ben and what had almost happened to me. And then life would be normal again, almost natural.

Marty raised her hand, put it flat against the glass. Her voice was muffled but I still heard her clear as daylight because she'd already as good as told me once. "You've got one lifeline, Hank, no breaks in it. Use it and be done with it. Remember."

My fingers uncurled—I didn't even remember knotting them to make a fist—and I put my hand flat on the other side of the glass. My hands were bigger than Marty's even though I was shorter. Jenny had liked that, that I was a girl with big hands. I shook my head. None of that got to matter anymore. "I'll remember." It was as good as a promise. I wanted to tell her to take care of herself but that was too close to what Ben had told me. There were other things unsaid—things that were always going to be unsaid because neither Ben nor I were around to say them anymore. We'd neither of us planned to leave her, never planned to leave Wanton.

Marty turned and gave me her back, but she didn't walk away for as long as I stood there. That was something. That was all the sign she was going to give me that she wouldn't entirely ignore that I'd ever existed since her plan to protect us hadn't worked.

It had to be my choice to go, no matter all the advice she'd given. I backed away until I hit the end of the porch, and then I turned around to go down the steps. More of those railroad ties. How had Marty had moved them there—or maybe it had been her daddy? Either way, they'd been solid. I walked, conscious of my back and shoulders the way Ben had been. I wasn't a man, never would be, but I could walk like one the way he had on his way to that big blue car, even as the storm rolled in to hide my tracks from anyone that bothered looking.

My bones felt strange, tight and stretched between my joints like I was being pulled inches taller with every step between the porch and the driveway. The wind made my skin feel a size too small, still hot even with the water in it, like the inside of a laundry room. The grass brushed my knees, and I walked beside the driveway around to the front of the house. Foot in front of foot in front of foot.

The rain started in real earnest then, all in a rush with a crack of lightning. It soaked my hair and my clothes and made me feel heavier. I paused at the end of the driveway. Ben had been carried off to the right. Toward the city. I turned left. Deeper country. I headed for trails that were soft dirt. They'd be nothing but puddles in this rain, but the water would drain off fast, leaving the old worn tracks in the scrub and the brush that grew up uncontrolled to guide my feet.

CHAPTER SEVEN

The Pantry Door Is Always Open

The first night, I slept in the middle of a clearing; I was already soaked and didn't want to get struck by lightning. And nothing much moved when it rained, so I wasn't afraid of anything hungry. I stomped down a bunch of tall grass to use for a bed. My backpack was a half-decent pillow. I felt numb, like the dark couldn't touch me anyway, too beat up by what had happened at Marty's place—not home, not anymore.

When I jerked myself awake, the ground had soaked up all the rain from during the night. The grass was green, not the dried up tan it had been but juicy and sweet when I broke off a stalk and chewed on it to get rid of the taste of my morning breath. In the early light, things didn't seem so bad—being out of doors was special in the morning, getting to listen to everything else waking up along with me. And the way the sky changed, lighting up from purple to blue, felt like it was happening just for me, for the very first time.

The second night, I slept under an old stone bridge over a creek that was barely a trickle even after the downpour. The bridge was half-collapsed and covered in hanging moss, grayer than the stonework. My hands shook as the light faded, but I leaned back against the supports that were still upright and felt sheltered just a little bit, just enough. It made me think of one of the stories Marty had told Ben and me when we were little.

"Trip, trap, trip, trap, who's that crossing my bridge?" I kept my voice soft, muttered the phrase, but the sound still made me flinch. I hadn't grumbled a word since leaving Marty's place. There had been no need for talking. We'd lived further out than just about anybody; everything after I turned left was all backcountry—scrub pine and palmetto.

The Three Billy Goats Gruff had been one of my favorites, all tense and scary. It was grisly, the first two billy goats eaten to pieces. But I had especially cheered for the third brother goat who had remembered to bring a chicken along with him for his walk, as a toll to offer the Reborn living under the bridge. That billy goat's survival had made everything seem more manageable—the dark of my bedroom wasn't outright friendly, but seemed like a thing I could reason with if ever there was a need. Trip, trap, trip, trap, right over the Reborn's bridge just because that billy goat had thought ahead.

This wasn't that kind of darkness, inside darkness. This was outside dark, and it made different noises. I had no chickens and I might not be as smart as that billy goat with his wily, sharp hooves dancing on the stones above my head. I longed for the chicken coop with a powerful fierceness, blinked away my memory of those bloody feathers and concentrated on the warm brooding bodies, their contented clucks and soft fat sides.

I pulled on one of my long-sleeved shirts and closed my eyes against it all. If Ben were here, he'd put me up on the stones above and stand where I was now and make growling noises like he was going to come eat me. He probably wouldn't eat me for real, wouldn't be at that point yet even if he hadn't escaped James and his coworkers. Ben was a real person and not a billy goat at all. It had only been one whole day, plus a little bit. We'd gone a whole day without eating before, when we were out exploring in the woods. We got hungry, but it wasn't so bad. And Marty had always had dinner waiting when we got back. Chicken and dumplings. Sausage and cabbage. Beans and rice. My mouth just about watered.

My food sack was only a little bit lighter—I had been careful yesterday and made do with some cheese and a little bit of the jerky—

so I didn't feel bad opening it up to dig out an apple. It'd be fine for dinner. Thinking about James, I wasn't hungry anyway.

The night made good sounds at least. It was louder than I expected it to be, all the other living things. Made me feel a little less lonesome. Easier to sleep, too, even though the ground under the bridge wasn't nearly as soft as my mattress at Marty's place and there was no one there to say goodnights back to me.

I woke up covered in dew. The bridge and moss had kept the ground I was on in the shadows so the sun was already up, but the air under the stone was still cool and damp. Not a bad way to wake up. The birds made a lot of morning racket, and that seemed like a good sign to me, if I had been one to believe in omens. Marty hadn't raised us to be superstitious, but I was learning how to be in a hurry.

Getting my things together was simple. Walking the rest of the way to where I was headed wasn't so much. It took hours. We had always stopped at the real tree line, where the woods got thick. That was where the roads gave out—Ben's old truck with its bald tires couldn't make it through the sand and dirt, and it didn't feel safe on foot. The trees grew too close, and their branches were too low, stubborn hardwoods mixed in with the pine trees, and live oaks sprawling in wherever they could stretch. I shouldered my bag—still full of sandwiches and dried fruit— and stepped into the mess of it.

It was cooler there in the shade of those trees, that was the first thing I noticed. Not just a little bit—enough that I almost shivered at the difference and a wave of goosebumps marched straight up my arms. I hadn't gotten far that first night in the rain, and then I'd walked in the sunlight the next day. It'd been hot, but I'd known where I was going and how to get there. The storm had broken the dry spell, and it was humid, sticky with bugs and sweat, and it felt like walking through some kind of fog. The air was outright oppressive and hard to take deep breaths of. My skin was as soggy and dirty as if I'd rolled in mud.

My boots did a good job protecting my feet, but the reflected light off the sand that was everywhere hurt my eyes, made the rest of my body sore, made me want to put my pack down and stretch out in the sun for a nap for a while. But I hadn't given in to the temptation—there weren't any safe places to sleep in the open when it didn't rain, I knew that much.

Marty had said surviving was a good enough goal. What I wanted to do first was find a safe place in the woods. A place where I could hole up, and take stock, and get a little rest that wasn't covered in damp. I might be okay then, at least for a little while. It'd be best if I could find the river—that'd be clean water and food both. I just had to stay alive and hidden long enough to find it. There had to be some place that would work.

If the birds singing at me to wake up that morning had been a good omen, the walking-over-my-grave feeling I got crossing the tree line negated all of it. I wasn't sure where to start reading the conflicting signs.

I really had no other plan though. There wasn't any place to go. It wasn't like I could hide in town or in Jenny's daddy's barn. I bit my lip against my longing for that barn, the hay loft all sweet smelling and lazy. I'd have even smiled to see Laura, been nice and polite to her like I never was.

But this was what I had—a bunch of trees growing up around me. Probably getting taller even as I stood there dithering about what to do next and remembering what I couldn't have anymore. I stepped further into all the different layers of shade, ghosts of trees fading out when the sun couldn't reach the ground to cast a shadow. Once I started walking, it got easier. Until my foot struck a root, and I caught myself against a rough trunk before I fell—maybe easier wasn't the right word for it after all. Wouldn't be a good idea to tempt fate in here.

The branches all crossed over each other, fought back against the light. There weren't as many pine trees, but needles carpeted the ground just the same, made my feet quiet among the leaves I couldn't identify. Every step was a shushing sound, like a mother with a fussy baby. Shush, shush, hush now, baby, mama's got you. Everything about my footsteps made me want my own mother, long-dead, and I twisted the ring on my finger.

The dirt, exposed in patches, was thick and black, rich soil instead of just plain dirt. Soil with nutrients for growing things, for protecting roots, instead of sand that let all the water drain out.

With my next step, my foot landed on a stick—a pile of sticks is what it felt like as dry wood splintered and crackled. The noise was so loud against the stillness of the woods, my hush-a-bye shuffle no kind of real disturbance.

That was wrong. There should be other noises, more living things, breathing things. There should be animals, birds especially. There was nothing truly silent in nature—Ben had been the one to tell me that, not Marty. But the deeper I walked, the further into the coolness of it all—the thicker the silence got until even the ground held onto my footsteps and I was left with my lungs rasping, drawing in air and pushing it back out.

My belly was too tired and tense to grumble about its emptiness. I stopped, leaned back against a tree trunk. The bark caught at my skin through the thin fabric of my shirt, held on to me. This was as good as any other place to stop for a minute. I slid to the ground, my shirt riding up until I grabbed it and pulled it back into place.

I felt so heavy and tired, despite my earlier conviction against nap taking. I closed my eyes and concentrated on my heartbeat steadily pumping blood all through my body, to every organ. Keeping me alive and on the track of my lifeline. Keeping me just a regular person, and I was grateful for that at least.

Then another stick cracked. But it wasn't my foot on the pile; I hadn't moved. The sharp retort of it offered a concrete rejection of the quiet. I tried to react, fast like every instinct I had screamed at me to do. But my eyelids moved at their own pace, opened slow and easy like it was a Sunday morning, and nothing I could do would make them move any faster. They slid, heavy and slow with wanting to sleep, over my eyeballs until finally everything focused.

The Reborn blurred like a heat vision in front of me, wavy and sharp. He—I assumed it was a he, but it could have been a woman once. The patches of hair clinging to the exposed, dingy white skull were short and faded, a dark red like auburn left to burn in the stove too long. Cinnamon sprinkled on milk, floating in lazy drifts.

He still stood there. I didn't want to look at the eye sockets, but when I did, every detail was very crisp, still had flesh around them, dry and fragile looking. He had blue eyes, watery blue like an old grandfather's eyes. Or, at least, what I imagined an old grandfather's eyes to look like. The Reborn wasn't looking at me. He stared with his comfortable old man eyes at a branch well above my head, high up in the tree. My head tilted back—I fought the movement; I didn't want to take my eyes off of him or draw his attention. But still my head tipped back until my crown was almost flat against the tree trunk and I could make out whatever he was looking at.

A squirrel. The first animal I'd seen since crossing into the deep woods, and I hadn't even heard it sitting there listening to the nothing. I shouldn't have been surprised at that though—the squirrel was frozen in place worse than I was, like it had never imagined moving before, staring back at the Reborn.

It made sense there weren't any other critters—not with a hunter, a predator like that moving around.

The Reborn finally stirred himself. He crept, slow enough that even though I was looking for it, I barely caught on to his movement. He was just suddenly in a different spot without rushing about it, nice and smooth. Lethal. He didn't blink. The squirrel stayed where it was, but it started to quiver. It wanted to run, even I could see that, get to the safety of another tree or a higher branch, but it was held in place by the power of the Reborn's gaze, the forcefulness of its hunger.

If he kept his direction, he was going to bump that strange invisible creeping right into me. I had to move. I'd make a better meal that the squirrel, so while I found the room to feel bad for it being paralyzed in its gaze, I couldn't spare being interested in buying his freedom with my own.

Marty had kept us out of the church, but she'd taught us to pray. Not like Seymour prayed in his big tent with the town folk all watching. Just quiet, in secret sometimes, by ourselves, a conversation with someone too far away to hear if they answered. She only ever mentioned it now and again, knocking soft and light when I was in bed, cracking my bedroom door open to wish me good sleep and ask if I'd remembered to say my prayers. I mostly had only done it when I was still afraid of the dark. Ben, though, he had prayed every night, he told me he did. I heard him at it sometimes, too, and then heard his deeper voice answering Marty when she asked him the same question. For all the good it did him. For all the good it had done any of us.

That wasn't a generous thought. But I'd found better uses for my hands than folding them once the lights went out. They weren't going to earn me forgiveness, especially when I didn't think I'd done much of anything wrong.

I prayed now though. Without thought or planning or making any conscious decision. My lips moved without making any noise, cracking as they shaped words I hadn't formed in that configuration for years. "Please, God, bless me that I might escape notice and that I will stay blind. Bless me that one life will be plenty and enough."

The Sight was supposed to run in families. Marty figured I had it. James went and carted Ben off for having it. The only things I'd ever seen out of the corners of my eyes had been town girls in thin dresses. Gauzy fabric to keep them from sweating in the summer, and the light shining right through. "Please, God, let me not See."

There was nothing else to do. I shifted my weight to my knees with the speed of molasses on a cold morning. I held my breath as I inched, didn't even inch, crept in fractions of inches, the way the Reborn had or as close as I could manage to approximate it. He was moving faster than me now, and still didn't make any noise at all. I spared a heartbeat to be impressed by that. But he was getting closer to my tree and to that squirrel. I kept up with my edging away, even though my insides wanted to leap out; my instincts told me fleet retreat would be the best option, but my brain knew better than my guts. He got closer but I kept it slow, until my back was to the tree that was now between us.

Staying alive was a good goal, a better one, a harder one than I'd thought. A very serious goal. I had been stupid the past few days, not thinking about this ahead of time. It wasn't like the Reborn were only out west, and it was inevitable that I'd actually see one. They had come, and they had stayed, and they'd made more of themselves the natural way, eating their loved ones. As hard as my first two days were, they were nothing compared to realizing that I needed to be logical, way more logical than I had been. I'd run on fear until there was nothing but a tree trunk between me and ending up turned.

I had to put more distance between us. I wanted to drop to my belly, but that'd just spread me out over the noisy leaves. Better to stay on my knees and go slow enough that he'd never notice me, never hear a thing. I just had to manage it.

He had long legs. Either that or there was something shifting and really weird about the way his pelvis sat. He probably just had really long legs. Fingers crossed. The rags of pants didn't make it to his knees on the right side and were even shorter on the left. Maybe they'd been his best dress trousers once upon a time, maybe he'd even borrowed them from someone so he'd look fancy. I couldn't tell if they were meant to be that shade of charcoal gray or if they were just dirty. Funeral dirt. From his grave.

One of his arms was extended now, worn down enough that the space between the bones of his forearm gaped clear. The ulna and the radius, Marty had taught us out of an old science book she had. We'd gotten extra lessons at home, from all of Marty's books. The pages were fragile with age, but the diagrams seemed accurate enough when I squeezed Ben's arm to feel the two bones. And now I was seeing them, more vivid than I'd imagined.

There were two trees between us now, my slow and careful knee walking carrying me further at a steady pace regardless of my muscles screaming at me to take off running. I took a few deep breaths on the backside of that second tree, leaned my forehead against its bark just to feel something for that wasn't the sweat that had gathered under my arm, swimming down my side every drop like a minnow. Not even a minute and I set off again.

Three trees. The Reborn was traveling, too. His arm led the way and then, though it was worse than seeing him move without moving, he was scrambling up the trunk of the tree—and I couldn't look away from anything, couldn't look away from the muscles he had left, and the bone, and the swinging of his rags as the air itself resisted him. We all knew they were dangerous, but as to how quick and agile they'd be? Who could say but any who'd survived a visit? And there weren't many of those going around and talking.

The Reborn climbed like an animal, all momentum and purpose, his fingers curved, bare worn finger bones digging into the trunk like sharpened claws. No fingernails, they had probably been one of the first things to fall away when he started losing the excess of his body.

The squirrel was fighting now, jerking back and forth even though the Reborn had yet to break its gaze. The fluffy little flag of a tail flailed back and forth, thrashing, and the bile rose in my throat.

There was a stick under my right knee—it registered before I put my weight down on it. I settled on my left knee instead and shifted to avoid it. The ground was softer here, more of that loamy black soil that smelled like the whole earth ready to grow things. I couldn't commit to a path until I knew where I was going, so I held fast with four trees between us, the Reborn halfway up the trunk now, closing in on that poor squirrel. I scanned the area ahead of me out of the corners of my eyes, right and left and front and back, keeping my focus on what he was doing, too.

Green leaves gave way to brown twigs, and those opened into a clear trail cut narrow enough that I hadn't seen it before, hadn't been at the right angle with the proper motivation. It could have been a deer path except for the way it was straight and cleared higher than a deer was tall. I looked back again, The Reborn had the squirrel in his hands and—I closed my eyes tight. I didn't want to watch that, couldn't stand to see it feed, all hunger and eagerness and blood and fur.

What I should have done was to plug my ears with my fingers. But I didn't think of that until the desperate rodent sound had already reached me, already set the hairs on my arms and neck up for attention and shivering at the pitch of it. That's what broke me—sent me running for the trail, just a few paces away. My feet were loud in the underbrush, twigs snapping like firecrackers, my traitor heart beating louder than all of that. It was a short distance, but my blood became all I could hear in my ears, waiting for the Reborn to shimmy down the tree and on top of me before I could realize it, looking for a juicier meal, something tender.

The trail was narrower than I thought, green wood catching at my hips and tearing at my hair as I ran. The branches could be claws; there was no way I'd know the difference until it was too late, until I was a meal in someone's gullet.

Unless he didn't kill me—that squirrel had still been alive, hadn't started screaming right off the bat. Would I make a sound like that, with teeth in my innards?

The hot moisture on my cheeks only registered when the salt of it stung at the welts left from crashing through the greenery. I ran until I couldn't anymore, my bags jangling and bumping against my back and my butt until my arms were fair to falling off from holding on to them so tight.

And then I held myself up, leaning against a tree because I couldn't stand on my own anymore, was bound to fall over, and then I wouldn't be able to pick myself up. I couldn't slow my breathing, couldn't catch my breath with a damn butterfly net if I'd had one.

It took more heartbeats than I was willing to count before the world flowed back into my ears like coming back from underwater. The silence of the woods was all around again, this time punctuated by birds chirping and bugs chittering, and I could smell the sap of the tree I was leaning against. Everything was normal; it was all what was missing when I'd noticed how quiet it was earlier. It couldn't sound like this, couldn't feel like this if that thing were after me.

I hadn't made it as far as I'd planned, but I reckoned I'd gone far enough for the day. I dropped my bags to the ground; I'd have lied to anyone who asked and told them this was a fine shelter spot, but the truth was, I didn't feel so steady and couldn't make it another step of travel.

Just the notion of it made me want to go to my hands and knees so I could throw up in peace.

Once we'd gone to live with Marty, we hadn't traveled much of anywhere. Not back to the city, that was for sure. Not out to its high-walled suburbs. Town was good enough for us, and we had just about everything we needed—the fields, and the animals, and Ben had hunted sometimes for more meat. I already missed it. It had been easy and good, and the tears sprang to my eyes again at how deep the emptiness in my chest felt when I thought about it.

Instead of letting myself sob like a baby—I wanted to just let the water out of my eyes until they were swollen and sore, and maybe I really would throw up from crying so hard—I sat down cross legged and put the heels of my hands to my eye sockets. I pressed hard enough to see colors on the inside of my eyelids. It had been fun, once, to do that when I was meant to be sleeping, to press and press until it was like fireworks, like explosions, and the afterimages had lingered even when I blinked my eyes open to see if I could see. I never could.

That third night I spent curled up under a shrub on the edge of the trail. It was warm enough. But that squirrel screamed its way all through my nightmares.

The woods were bigger than I'd realized. I managed a pretty straight path, at least I thought I did, and started leaving marks for myself, planning ahead, just in case. But I still hadn't found the river, and everything was starting to look the same. I hadn't doubled back on any of my marks by late on the fourth day, so I kept walking. The birds and the other animals kept making noise. I was in a daze, hypnotized by my own regular pace. Things made sense: the less I ate, the longer my food supplies would hold. But the less I ate, the worse I felt, the worse shape I'd be in to deal with it when my supplies inevitably ran out. I tried to pay more attention to my surroundings, tried to remember the woodcraft Ben had taught me. Tried to prepare, but my eyes always drooped, and I stumbled along like a sleepwalker.

And so, on the fifth night, I ate my last scraps of cheese.

CHAPTER EIGHT

Always Carry A Chicken When You Cross A Bridge

For all our exploring and big talk about dare-deviling, Ben and I had never camped out. That was for fools telling fairytales. I'd heard people talk about the concept, a few braggarts making wild claims not to be believed in the first place. But it did seem like the kind of thing a boy wanting to prove he was a man would do—with no real understanding, especially if that boy was from town, of how easy it was to lose your way in the wilderness.

Now I caught myself wishing I had paid more attention to those stories. The mornings out of doors were growing on me, but I didn't have a lot of skills when it came to making my living direct from the same land I slept on. I had to figure it out quick though.

My marks on the trees kept me going about in the right direction—north. South would have just taken me to more little towns like Wanton, and as much as the familiarity might have made me breathe easier, it felt like letting myself get cornered. Plain east would have put me in the ocean eventually, but it was a hell of a long walk away. Same for heading west. I would have admitted my inexperience to anyone around, but I wasn't a damn fool, at least I didn't think so. Ambitious traveling plans could come after I'd figured out more of the survival thing.

What I needed was more land around me, not more land to cover. That meant north as well as east, heading to some place that wasn't the same old place. I hadn't always lived in Wanton, but I might as well have for all my conscious mind remembered.

I trudged along, my parents keeping pace with me. My mother, really. The clearest in the few memories I had. If I started with the way she smelled, more details came to me. Always floral with a hint of baby powder, to keep from sweating in the heat of day, though it wasn't she but Marty who had taught me to powder my crotch and armpits and around my small breasts to avoid heat rash and chaffing. My mother had dark hair like mine—maybe. My mental image of her was black and white, fuzzy around the edges like I was remembering a photograph rather than a real person.

That might have been the case. Marty had one photo of my parents, their wedding picture, hanging in the hallway. The two of them had been smiling at the corners of their mouths, trying to take a proper serious photo and failing, my father's eyes looking toward my mother instead of at the camera. It always made me think they'd loved each other, that they'd have had to love us. And maybe understood us, too, understood why Ben flirted and why I told stories. I wasn't complaining about Marty, certainly, but sometimes I wondered.

Which didn't distract me from the most important thing I needed to find—some kind of regular supply of clean water. Without it, I wouldn't last more than a few days, especially in the heat. I was already a little cotton-mouthed. At least, my skin hadn't already dried out. And I didn't have the runs. I wasn't prissy, not by much measure, but having the shits in the woods made me squirm in my skin with a different kind of horror. Squatting with a hand on a tree trunk for balance was already bad enough.

I should have packed a canteen. Hindsight nibbled at my heels, told me how much better off I'd have been if I hadn't rushed out in such a hurry. I didn't want to think about it, but—why had Marty been in such a rush? I didn't like any of the reasons I came up with. The truth was that she'd hurt my chances. Survive, she'd all but commanded—and then set me off in the dark without any way to defend or even feed myself. At least she'd put the storm at my back like a broom to cover my tracks.

Survive, she'd all but begged, and then pushed me out like James had been banging on the front door while we stood at the back. There had to have been something else; she had to have known something. Especially since she'd sent me deeper into the country, away from the tracks that could have led me in a straight line right up to where I could try to hop a train.

With a few simple words, she'd made me question everything she'd told me about my parents. It made everything else suspect, too. I figured she'd been threatened; had they, whoever they were, told her they'd kill her? Take her in our places? Shouldn't she have stood firm, anyway?

Nothing good was coming of me thinking like that. My shoulders were sore and low from it already. I shook my head and focused on what was in front of me, not what was behind. The river. That was the first order of business, and it *was* around here someplace. I might have veered further west than I intended, but I'd been checking the sun in the morning, to make sure I could correct for any drifting during the day.

And it was raining every afternoon, short bursts of furious water. I hadn't been able to rig anything to catch and keep it, but I opened my mouth to collect the drops.

After the rain was the worst. Wet through to my skin, with soggy clothes, I almost steamed in the afternoon sun. I couldn't smell my own stink from sweat and dirt, too deep in it to scent myself. Maybe it wasn't as bad as I thought. Maybe the rain kept me clean. I'd worry about it if I ever saw any humans again, instead of just birds and lizards and the odd startled deer.

If I spent the rest of my life wandering around lonely, it wouldn't really matter.

Once I figured out water, I'd need to worry about food, too. I could go longer without that than I could go without water, but it wasn't really in my best interests. I could probably figure out a snare to catch squirrels. But it might be a while before I could eat squirrel without thinking of that Reborn. The screaming was still clear as anything in my ears, drowning out even Marty's last words to me if I weren't careful about stuffing the noise of it back down.

My progress slowed down; walking meant checking the ground for mushrooms and other greens. It meant listening for the sounds of water or of animals rustling away. Taking a slower pace also made the going a little easier, and I filed that away as important: the more I rushed, the harder it was to make progress, the longer things seemed to take. The scrub fought my feet, but I could work my way through it if I just took a second to look where I was going first.

It was probably a mistake to feel optimistic. But I couldn't right help myself.

The humidity that had brought on the storm disappeared as the afternoon progressed; by the time the sun went down, the air was dry enough to hold a little bit of uncharacteristic chill. I slept curled up and wearing all my shirts.

In the morning, the dust started to settle.

So much dust—it was finer than the gray dirt I was used to, finer than the piles of sand all around. It had a reddish cast, and my eyes watered from the sting of it. It made my throat hurt, and I pulled the collar of my t-shirt up over my nose as the sun hit its high point.

With every step, I held my breath in hope. I looked, started at all the green places, all the leaves and the scrub. Everything looked fresh, but looks weren't what was true. Marty had taught us all the signs. Storms were usually either all bluster and blow or rain. But the last dust storm that had come through, she'd called us into the house in the middle of the afternoon, barred the door and made us sit, tight together, in the closet in the center of the house. She'd draped heavy wet blankets over us and I'd protested, the air too hot and stagnant under there. She'd almost slapped me—she had never come close to that before.

It took a while, but we'd settled, and I'd stopped my complaining. The noise of the wind rose up and, even in our closet, hiked up the air pressure until it felt like our ears had been stopped up by cotton balls. The light seeping around the crack under the door disappeared. Once that little bit of shine was extinguished, I'd realized what real darkness was.

It wasn't the noise of a thunderstorm crackling and striking over our roof. It was more like a hurt cat and a woman gone mad with grief tearing at her hair. It was wailing, low and long. The wood beams of the house creaked and moaned, added to the injury.

Even with that, I'd fallen asleep, hot breath puffing against the inside of my arm, moist and clammy. We'd stayed in there until morning, until the light had come back. I halfway expected we'd need to call for help fixing the house, but there hadn't been much damage.

What there had been, everywhere but especially in drifts well up the side of the house and the fence and anywhere else there was something to lean against, was dust.

Marty had told us not to touch it. The folks in town had swept it all up and fertilized the fields with it by the time we made it back to the general store—no one liked to leave dust laying around and superstition was that the dust was rich in the basic elements of life. Better that go to the plants than get in anyone's nose. My feet stuttered as I remembered: Marty had spread ours on the field the cucumbers had grown in.

Even if it couldn't turn anybody on its own, the dust was queer; it was the reason things had changed, the reason the Reborn rose. And they were more active after a storm, regardless of how they had been made; the wind stirred them up, got them moving and hunting. Hell, maybe it made them thirsty, and they were just trying to slack that parched feeling. There were plenty of theories and none of them sounded more likely than another.

I'd thought about it sometimes, though, when we were binging on water after working the fields and my throat was dry and gritty and my hands—gray and dirty until I washed off in the sink.

No easy sink to get myself a drink from or to clean up in out here. No closet to hide in. No wet blanket to shield myself with, for that matter. The scrub whipped back and forth, telling me all about the pace of the wind that was swirling around and making me kick up my pace even though it'd dehydrate me faster. I wadded up my t-shirt's neck and stuffed it in my mouth, pulled it out as wet with spit as I could get it and held it over my nose, a makeshift dust mask.

There was a group of pines up ahead. But for every step I took, the wind kicked up another notch and the temperature dropped another degree. My arms prickled and when I managed to focus on them, I realized they crawled with gooseflesh. A shiver rumbled my shoulders and I looked up—the sky was getting dark and green. I'd seen it that color before, usually in the fall, when the hurricanes would try to wipe us all up from where we spilled across the land. Against the eerie light, the dust caught in my arm hair looked bright red. I broke into a half run. Pine trees weren't as sturdy as hardwoods but they would do better than nothing.

I slapped a hand against the first trunk I reached—the back of it bit into my palm. The little pain caught my breath for me. I forged a little deeper into the trees, then let my knees buckle with my back to one and my front to a palmetto bush, all sharp leaves and sturdy stems. I tried to duck under the palmetto and still keep my back to the pine tree. My bag went under my knees, crammed between my calves and thighs, then I wrapped my arms around my legs as tight as I could so I was a little round ball, as small as I could get myself. The whine of the storm turned up and the weird-colored light went clean out, like someone had flipped a generator switch and cut all the power.

There was just enough time—I loosened myself up to tuck my head all the way inside my shirt, and then shrank myself again, closed my eyes, and tried to count.

Numbers didn't mean much of anything—all I could think about was that my arms were still bare and even though I had the tree to my back, dust and grit and I didn't even know what all already scraped and pulled at my skin as it shifted in the wind. I'd be smooth as a plank if I lasted through the storm. Even if I didn't.

Maybe I wouldn't even have any skin left, just red and white and muscle and sinew—like the Reborn and maybe that was how they were really made in the first place. Not the dust and the way it filled up your lungs, but the dust and how it stripped off all of your body like a bad suit.

Inside my shirt, with my eyes squeezed closed, the rising dust tickled my mouth, my nose. Dry and not from around here—it didn't have the fertilizer tang of our fields or the chalky taste of the gray dirt that made us filthy at the end of a day. This was minerals—iron and rust and old things that should have been left where they were to begin with. I'd lost three baby teeth at the same time when I was little, and Marty had made me hold a penny in my mouth. The copper had made my teeth ache. This reminded me of that, like there was a current running through me and testing all the different frequencies.

My throat spasmed, and I fought back a cough, struggled to hold on to my spit. I couldn't waste the moisture in the middle of a storm. Everything around overwhelmed me until I couldn't hear my own heartbeat, though it had to be loud, it beat so fast. I relaxed my jaw and let the saliva pool under my tongue even as something caught my hair and pulled free, taking strands of me with it, making my scalp burn.

Once upon a time, I told myself. Once upon a time, there had been a chicken named Chicken Little. And Chicken Little had pecked her way around the barnyard every morning, finding her breakfast. Until one day, Chicken Little pecked her way right over to an old live oak tree. And, before she knew it, an acorn had fallen and smacked her right on the beak, in between her little bitty black eyes. Chicken Little wasn't very smart—she'd run right back to the coop as fast as her little legs could carry her, flapping and clucking and carrying on. The sky was falling, she told everyone who had half a mind to listen to a fool chicken. The sky was falling and the end was nigh.

Even though the wind was picking up speed around me and I shivered from the cold, I tried to keep my breathing shallow and regular. Calm, calm, calm. I just had to stay right where I was, just had to ride it out. The dust didn't turn anyone, and getting it on me was just going to get me dirty.

I kept on with my story. Marty's voice whispered in my ear, even over the wail of the wind. Chicken Little had told everyone the end was coming and they'd better repent—and some had listened to her and some hadn't. Nothing happened to any of them though, and nothing happened to Chicken Little because it had been an acorn, not the sky falling. And so the next day, she'd gotten back up and gone pecking around until she'd found herself back under that old oak tree again. This time, instead of clocking her on the face, an acorn pegged her right on her tail feathers. Chicken Little went running again, right back to the coop, clucking and carrying on again. This time there weren't half as many with a mind to listen to her.

She'd bent their ears anyhow, preaching and prying into their business. Some of the other animals, mostly the geese, had taken her as seriously as she took herself. But at the end of the day, the same thing was true as the day before—nothing happened and all the sinners and repenters sat together in the barnyard.

When Marty told us the story, Chicken Little had carried on the same for three or four more days. The chicken got a little more bruised, a little more tenderized every time until she'd have been just the thing for a Sunday dinner. But even though she was a foolish little biddy, she weren't entirely without smarts. And so Chicken Little, one fine morning, headed off in the opposite direction in search of her breakfast and avoided that old oak tree entirely. She didn't have to understand the end of the world to prevent it.

And the world hadn't ended either way. She'd kept on pecking for her breakfast in every retelling I'd ever heard. Marty'd used it as a bedtime story, but there was no going to sleep now, not with my knees for a pillow and the creaking pine trunk as a bed frame.

If I were a little bug, fat and juicy and crawling around in the green grass, Chicken Little would have eaten me for her breakfast. But even then the world wouldn't have ended. Once that clucker learned to stay away from the damn tree, the world made sense again.

I didn't have to understand the end of the world. I just had to stay out of its way. I just had to keep breathing.

Storms could go on for days—I'd read that in a book of Marty's, but she hadn't needed a book to predict the weather. And she probably didn't. I wasn't as learned as her so I'd read everything I could in it. I wouldn't last for days—I'd choke to death on dirt if that happened, my nose already full of grit under my shirt.

Choking on dust wouldn't be pretty—and then I probably would come back, regardless of what folks believed, hungry and not even knowing my name. I cracked my eyes open, just enough so I could blink.

Some of the light was starting to come back. It was just as cold and my arms felt wet—and sliced open from the palmetto. But the wind wasn't shrieking so loud. Hurricanes had eyes and if it had just been rain, I'd have figured that's where I was, in the momentary calm of the center. But dust clouds rolled over like a wave, covered you and dragged you down in the undertow before they crashed down and went on past as they traveled to the sea.

I'd been feeling optimistic right before the storm hit. Feeling that way now seemed like an invitation to further disaster. I shoved my hope away, kept my head down. I waited.

Figuring out the time wasn't my strong suit on a good day—I was too impatient to be real accurate. Now time didn't matter at all. I counted again, this time to keep my breathing steady, my heartbeat regular. I focused on every number until I couldn't even hear the wind, couldn't feel the wet, couldn't spare a thought about how I was going to get the knots out of my hair. Things zoomed past me, but as long as I was still, they weren't my concern.

I didn't have to care about the things happening around me—and nothing happened to me. I blinked, and it was dark again. But not the unnatural dark—I could tell the difference now—of the sun being blocked out by a dust cloud. This dark was easier, not so absolute even under the trees. I blinked again. It had to be night. If that was the case, I needed to move, needed to find a place to sleep. But my arms stayed locked around my legs, and I stayed where I was.

The next time I blinked, there was light creeping in through the fabric of my shirt.

Morning. It had to be. I forced my neck to straighten, and this time my body obeyed. My head popped out of my shirt and my muscles protested, ached at the change of position. I winced—standing up was going to hurt. But sitting hurt, too, now that I was paying attention. Everything still looked fuzzy, and I reached up to wipe at my eyes. My arms felt like lead, and they moved *slow*. My fingers were swollen up in protest of bending. What I could see of my skin was dusty red, like I'd been rolling around in clay that had dried all over me. I worked my tongue, tried to summon up enough moisture to spit on my hands, get them a little clean before I rubbed my eyes. There wasn't enough to do more than dampen the insides of my cheeks. I coughed, choked hard enough that black spots danced in front of the blur that was still all I could really see.

I blinked again, then again, frantic, and my eyes finally watered. My vision started clearing up, and the details all sharpened. It wasn't just me covered in red; it was everything. All the plants that had been so green and wet were dried out and wore a coat of red. Some of the other palmetto bushes were outright buried. And with the sudden crispness of my sight, I saw a rabbit leg sticking out of one of the piles. I jerked back at that, the bite of the pine bark sharp enough through my shirt to ground me. I pushed back against it, hard, used the leverage to stand up on my protesting legs, then clung to the tree.

My legs just about gave out, my knees happy for the movement, but my thighs trembling so bad, I had to hold on tight to keep myself from sitting down faster than I'd stood up in the first place. Instead of just using the tree to steady myself under my own power, I leaned on it, depended on it to keep me on my feet.

I really should have brought a damn canteen. I could have used it. The dust had brought a harsh rasp to my breathing, like I'd swallowed a cactus and caught pneumonia from it. The knowledge that Marty had sure and certain probably on purpose sent me out ill-prepared sat heavy on my chest. Away from the cities, away from any help, no matter what she had implied about the cities not being safe for me. But there was no use hiding when there was no way to hide from the dust. She'd told me to survive, and then she'd sent me out to fail. I let myself consider what I hadn't since I'd left: what had she meant about my parents and her husband? Had she sent them out the same way she'd packed me off into the unknown? Had she been working with them or against them? For how long?

I was learning in spite of her, but nowhere near fast enough. And I was running short on choices, if I'd ever really had any to begin with. I rubbed my thumb against the ring on my finger and tried not to cry.

CHAPTER NINE

Good Fences

There were so many damn pine trees. When I pushed further into the stand of them that had sheltered me during the storm, they just never seemed to end. They grew in rows—some straight and some all out of line, zigzagging back and forth until you could make yourself dizzy trying to follow their lead with your feet. Mine, for one, didn't much care where they led me at this point, just as long as it featured no more pine trees.

My arms were a scratched-up wreck, fingers to armpits, from debris during the storm but also from fighting through saw palmetto that grew thick right up to the bases of the trees. There were clearings full of it, clustered tight until there was no way through but to step in the middle of it. None of the cuts were deep, but there were a lot of them, leaving me raw.

I'd changed into my long sleeves but the damage was already done.

Sweat dropped out of my hair and onto the ground where I was bent over, taking a break because I had to, my belly cramped up but not enough to distract me from what kept playing in my mind, clearer than when I stood there and watched it happen. I held on to the trick I'd learned during the storm, counting to keep my breathing deep and regular—every time I closed my eyes, my chest tightened and my lungs went shallow and fast like the aftermath of running away.

The corners of my eyes. That's where the Sight lived, where I had denied having anything at all except maybe a little bit of sass for Marty when I got to feeling impertinent. Extra vision, everyone said, when you needed it, even when you didn't need it. Maybe especially when you didn't. It made sure you saw everything, took in all the corners and the dead spaces in between where things happened. I'd only ever used my eyes to look at people, see what they were really like when they thought no one could see them. But I saw more than that when I looked at things now.

The Reborn had grasped the squirrel in one hand. The branch had sagged and swayed, but he had looked to be mostly bone. Bones and the rags of his clothing, someone's second-best suit once upon a time. His fingers, the ends sharpened to claws visible even from that distance because, at that moment, I could see everything, see his fist curled around the quivering meat as he raised it to his open, lipless mouth. He had sharp teeth, sharp as his fingers, sharp like carnivores', teeth meant to strip meat away from bone and connective tissue, meant to tear.

I'd broken and run because I couldn't stand to watch him feed, to see too much. But I'd already seen it all and I was never going to forget it, could never forget it with the way it kept replaying in my head every time I held still to let my heartbeat settle. The Sight wouldn't let a body forget. I'd run and prayed to escape, but that prayer had been a lie. I'd run because I was afraid he'd pull me in with that gaze, hypnotize me the way he had that squirrel until I saw my ruin coming for me and welcomed it the way those people had kissed the Reborn under Seymour's tent. I'd have stood still for it and waited.

It was enough rest. Especially if I was just going to sit around mooning about what was going on behind my eyelids, the horrible fissures in my brain. I couldn't afford that, not with the Reborn always more active after a storm. The trees were never going to end, but I trudged back into the thick of them, broke into something like a trot, as much as I could manage through the palmetto. When the scrub cleared out, I let my legs stretch my awkward hitching gait into a run.

I'd been out of food for two whole days, nothing left to carry but myself. I'd caught a little water when I could, and I still mostly felt okay, hungry but okay. And I was going to go stark raving loony like Lady Bird Jenkins back in Wanton, if I didn't do something that felt good.

I burst into another clearing, my pace holding me proud and high so I could breathe through my nose, which was more than I'd been able to do when I'd run away from that Reborn. The deer in the clearing startled, fled with bounding leaps as I broke through the bushes. Even so, the presence of another living thing was always going to be a comfort to me. Just like I couldn't forget any of the rest of what had happened, I couldn't forget the silence, the way all sound had disappeared as the animals fled or hid and the profound emptiness had smothered out all good sense.

The thought was enough to slow me, to make me stop. I doubled over, hit with a coughing fit I hadn't seen coming, hands on my knees and hacking up phlegm. Tears dripped off my nose, and that was the only reason I knew I was crying, wasting more water. I could still see just fine, but couldn't really feel anything except the numbness on my face.

My tears mingled with my snot and made me a regular mess. I'd be puffy and red. The brief elation had fled, left me hurting and hard-pressed to feel anything else. This wasn't going to work. No place was going to be safe enough. Marty had pushed me out that door on purpose, and I couldn't do this, couldn't stand up to her now any more than I'd been able to stand up to her when I was little.

The deer's head had been low. It had been drinking. I staggered over, expecting the small pool of water that I found. But it was more than that, and I stared more out of habit than real understanding for too long. It wasn't a pool so much as a wide spot in a little creek. A little creek that had to be shooting off from the river. And if it was safe for the deer, it'd be safe enough for me. In fact, that deer probably had better sense than me about where to find drinking water. I didn't much care at any rate, still too numb from hurting in my chest—I knelt, trembling, and splashed my face, did it again so I could scrub away the sweat and the snot, the dust and the dirt, the upset and the fear, at least for one minute.

The water was tangy, like kissing someone who'd just eaten an orange. It might have been how thirsty I was all of a sudden, my awareness of how dry I was roaring back, but it was the best water I'd ever tasted. I crouched, balanced with a hand on the bank so I could duck my whole head under; I needed to feel clean. I could head upstream toward the river and maybe clean my whole self, naked in the sunlight sparkling on the water's surface. I held my breath and stayed under as long as I could. I had seen too much; I had Seen.

If I didn't find food soon, food to go with this water, if my belly stayed empty, I would See more. It couldn't be avoided, it was just how things worked.

I pulled my head up, shook the water off my skin, out of my hair, like a dog fresh out of the river. I twisted and squeezed the ends of my ponytail—there wasn't even the snap of a twig to warn me but as wide as my eyes were open, I knew there was going to be a person, a figure watching me when I dropped my hair.

There was. She was tall. She'd be taller than me when I stood up from where I crouched on the bank. But she was alive, wasn't Reborn, ruddy skin, shiny with sweat, keeping her distance.

I held my breath. She might have held hers. My heart thudded until I worried she or I would scream from the heavy forbidding sound of it.

"I'm Hank." My voice was a saw on green wood, teeth all choked.

The silence broke like it was a real glass wall—the woods were still there full of living things, but there hadn't been anything between us but the feeling of a quiet and desperate struggle.

The air was too thick in my throat and I coughed again, had to drop back down onto one knee to have any hope of catching myself, making it stop. When I looked up, she was backing away, still on silent feet. I cried out, a wordless protest.

She paused, looked at me so that I felt it—I blushed to realize what she saw. I was half-drowned and still filthy, scratched-up and wearing too many layers for the heat. My hair was tangled, loose parts drenched and sticking to my forehead. My pants didn't feel any different so I was still round and shiny—I was awkward and sweaty and in, I figured, her backyard.

"What are you doing here?" Her voice was such a whisper, I could have mistaken it for wind through the tree branches if I hadn't been watching her mouth. If she walked around talking like that all the time, it was no wonder Billy, down at the service station on the other side of town, was convinced the woods were haunted.

There was no point in lying, even if I knew what lie to tell anyway. "I'm running and hiding, trying to stay safe." That was the gist of it, my still-forming plan to find shelter. I tried to keep my voice as soft as hers, as appealing. Marty'd told me not to let myself get caught unawares, but I was too desperate for contact.

The ease of her posture lent her something like age, but the more I looked at her, the more I was convinced she was probably only a lick and a hair older than me. More like Ben's age, maybe. Her hair was tied back and up, off her neck. Her clothes were manly, no skirts in the woods, just patched jeans, but she wore them well. Her muck-colored t-shirt looked old and soft from too many washings and skimmed her hips. Her features were strong, like a real fine building. Not exactly pretty in an easy way, but there was something that made me want to keep looking, just in case I could figure out what it was.

"We all are." She gave me her back again, but this time she gestured over her shoulder for me to follow. She even waited, as still and silent as she'd been since I first saw her, until I gathered up my senses along with my backpack and splashed through the creek, boots and pants wet through in the crossing, so I could stand at her side.

That must have been the right answer to a question she hadn't actually asked, to a question I didn't think I had the brains to understand in that moment anyway.

"What's your name?" I'd been right—she was taller than me. But not by all that much and so I held my back straight, kept my neck long and tall, her taking my measure without looking directly.

"You can call me Dell." She made that come-follow-me gesture again, a quick flick of her fingers. Her legs were longer than mine, ate up the distance, and I obeyed. She didn't make any noise at all, not even a soft rustle over the patches of leaves.

I watched her feet more than where we were going, trying to step in the same places she did. But I still came down too heavy, too sudden. I couldn't quite manage the rhythm of it, couldn't feel my way into the quiet spots like I had during my significant retreat. I only had one lifeline, Marty had said—but she hadn't looked at my right hand. She hadn't looked at the broken line there. And I did want my life to be longer than this, my bout of despair shocked out of me. I wanted to survive.

Dell didn't slow down even to minimize all the racket I made. She didn't look back at me though she knew I was there. She'd told me I could call her Dell—that meant it wasn't anything like her real name. Safer that way.

Marty had told us names had personal power, that nicknames were better for everyday use. That was why Ben was never Benjamin to either of us and why she'd dubbed me Hank. Also I hated being called Henrietta. So having a short name felt double fortunate to me.

Names could give you special influence over a person, could make them listen extra hard to you, could help you see them a little more clearly no matter what they tried to hide. I'd known Seymour's name, and I'd seen the fire in his eyes. If you knew the name of a Reborn, sometimes you could make them listen to you, make them do what you wanted. Maybe you could even make them live in a cage. Maybe—but maybe not, if the stories about Reborn coming back and finding their families first were true. I was so turned around, I didn't entirely know what to believe anymore.

And regardless, you still couldn't exactly reason with them. The Reborn had their own hungry logic, and the living couldn't really grasp it. But if you called a Reborn's whole entire name, gossip went, they'd see you and hear you, regard you as something other than food, more than just a pile of meat on the move.

I didn't know anyone who'd had a chance to test that theory. Hell, it wasn't anything most people wanted to run around trying out. Marty had sworn up, down, sideways, and backward that she'd seen it work, which may be how Seymour's whole group kept itself safe.

Names had power, which meant I had just handed over a chunk of it to Dell. Just a nickname on the surface, but it felt like a true name— it was what I called myself in my own head. And now she knew that, could work something with it if she wanted. When she'd told me what to call her, it had rung like a public name. No power there, everything a surface exchange.

Damn, I'd made a simple mistake. I added another lesson to my list—my mind might feel like molasses, I might feel like a child, but I needed to think before I spoke to people. Anyone else I met wasn't going to be my own folks, wasn't going to be someone I'd known and grown up learning. And not everyone was going to have good intentions. I couldn't take my name back from Dell, but as long as I didn't give it to anyone else from my own lips, well, I'd count that as progress. And maybe I'd make myself up a name in the meantime, a private name just for me. That would be a little bit of protection, especially if I didn't give it to anyone else.

Dell kept on with her walking, between trees and avoiding the worst of the scrub. She went deeper and deeper into the woods that didn't seem to end until I was surprised we didn't come out clean on the other side. We had to be going north—I kept glimpsing the river off to the side. I didn't think I'd been going in circles, so it was nice to have some confirmation that my plan had worked. I considered asking, but she kept a brisk pace and after what felt like a steady hour of walking, I wasn't sure I had the breath left to string together the words.

Didn't have the energy either, if I were being honest with myself. My stomach was cramping from the water, hurting more and more with every step. It had been so refreshing, but I'd had too much, too fast. The next time I squatted behind a tree, my shit was going to be runny and painful.

My misery had too strong a hold for me to notice at first, but then we walked through a patch of out-and-out sunlight that wasn't filtered through leaves and pine needles. The trees had thinned out for real this time, not just a too-brief clearing filled with sharp edges. It was a little bit of prairie, with tall grass and low wiry ground cover, tough and thick under my boots. I gave thanks—and in the spaces between the fog starting to settle down as the sun went south, I saw the fence.

Tall, metal, trimmed with the same razor wire that topped out chicken fence. I thought back to the coop, for once not just to that pile of feathers but to the regular motion of feeding the chickens, scattering seed by hand. Our razor wire hadn't kept the worse predators out.

I'd been blaming James, like he'd started it all. But maybe it had really started with those missing chickens, dinner in a hungry belly that wouldn't ever be sated. And maybe that meant it had started with Seymour, and the way his caravan couldn't have arrived so early in our front yard without having driven through the night. Like as not he'd done more than kiss that Reborn—maybe even opened that cage up and let the thing out to hunt.

The razor wire was the extent of the familiar about the fence. This one was made with metal slats, the spaces between each one narrow, just enough to let a little bit of wind whistle through. That made sense; it'd ruin the purpose of the enclosure in the first place if a good, stiff wind could blow it over—or if grasping fingers could work their way into it. In that sense, it really was a wall more than a fence. The razor wire draped over the top and had to hang down on the inside—as much to keep things in as it was to keep them out.

It gave me a shiver to look at it. But Dell walked right up to it, followed it like it was the trail she'd been looking for. I kept a further distance from it than she did but stayed right on her heels. She reached a hand out, ran a finger along the slats as we walked, making the metal ring dully. I watched her finger instead of my feet and counted every time her fingertip bumped over a gap.

I started at one. Two. Three. Four. Five. And then I caught my toe on a rock. I stumbled but Dell didn't even pause; when I caught myself, the distance between us had grown. Seven. Eight.

I kept counting, but also kept my eyes flickering back and forth from her finger to the ground because I was pretty sure she wasn't going to stop to help me up even if I fell on my face. She'd keep going wherever she was going, and if I fell behind, I'd lose her. Then I'd be left to whatever crawled up to this fence out of the woods at night.

By the time I reached a hundred and nineteen, I'd caught up a little bit. We turned a sharp corner—the corner stabilized by metal flashing that lapped over where the slats set at a right angle to each other met. At two hundred and seventy-nine, I noticed a break in the monotonous expanse of metal slats and gaps, but I couldn't tell what it was until four hundred and thirty-three. It was a gate. And it was open.

My breath, which I hardly had a hold of anyway in the dusky light, rushed out of me in a gasp. An open gate, and Dell showed every sign of going right inside it. The detail got clearer with every step—uniformed guards on each side, and their guns way fancier than Marty's old shotgun. Not quite like the state troopers who sometimes stopped in town to eat; I'd seen one or two over the years, sipping coffee on the porch at the general store. These uniforms were just as official though, and perfectly matched.

"I'm back from my rounds." Instead of the whisper she'd used on me back by the water, Dell's voice was as clear and loud as hitting a piano key. She produced a card from her back pocket, identification, most like. That made me bite the inside of my cheek—the only identification I had was a birth certificate and it was back in Marty's closet, where we'd always kept the important papers. I'd never even seen it.

The guard on the right didn't say anything, just nodded like he was bored and moved the barrel of his gun to let Dell in. He barred my way though, set the barrel across my path when I went to follow her. I flinched back—it had been too many days, just me and the wild things, and I'd never liked anyone grabbing at me anyway, especially in a crowd.

Before I could think of a smart remark, something defensive, Dell shook her head. "I found her by the water. She's a stray. I'm taking her to Granny's house," she said like that was the most natural thing in the world. And it must have been, because the gun moved away and the guard stepped aside, waved me into the compound. That was the only word I knew for it. This wasn't like town; I hadn't even read about a place like this. My shoulders were tight, uncertain as I moved closer to Dell, saw the way she and the guard still stared at each other, neither entirely willing to back down.

"I still need her name for the records. You know the rules." The guard wasn't being menacing to me anymore, but he wasn't welcoming either. The look he turned Dell's way was familiar—and stern. They'd had this fight before.

"Hank. I'm just Hank." My voice wasn't as clear as hers had been, still too used to grit and dryness and not having anybody to say anything to. I'd make up a private name, but I didn't have it in me to make something else up for public use. Now that we weren't walking, I felt heavy again, like my arms wanted to fall clean off. None of them knew my whole name, and that was going to have to be good enough.

Maybe. But I was so tired, and I couldn't find it in me to care about it anymore. Some of that must have shown on my face because the guard turned back to me, looked at me instead of Dell. His face softened as he took in my details. "You look like a tired out stray dog, Hank." He glanced at the other guard, waited for that man to nod. Then he waved me further in. "Be careful." He voiced it low as I passed him, and it was like walking straight into another world.

I followed Dell, but I glanced back at him. He watched us. I was knock-kneed with weariness, and didn't want to fall, so I turned forward again, kept up with Dell, and moved deep into the fog.

Wood houses, some with stone sides knocked together with walls and roofs. No windows. Lots of open doors, all of them at ground level. There were people, too, all coming and going, hardly glancing at me as we all walked through the haze. They were living. They were living like their lives were normal.

It made me cold. And I was afraid.

CHAPTER TEN

It Feels Like Safety

The deeper we got into the compound, the more people saw me. The more a few stared at me. The in-between folks drifting in and out of the small houses, the purposeful types moving like they had somewhere to be, the relaxed ones just sitting on their front step like they were welcoming the coming evening.

Town was mostly white. There were some folks darker than others, and it wasn't a big deal. But I'd never seen so many different kinds of folks in one place like this. Everyone had their own eyes, too—brown and blue and green and blind, milky white with fortune-telling in unlined faces too young for them.

Their suspicious curiosity thrummed against my skin. Not a lot of visitors, I was guessing.

No one wore any sort of badge or anything, but for all their differences, there was something the same about them, like they all got their clothes from the same place supplying the guard uniforms, like they all got their hair cut by the same barber. They looked like they belonged here, inside the fence.

I sure didn't have that look.

My feet dragged, but I kept pace with Dell, glad her footsteps slowed down some now that we had found ourselves smack in the middle of civilization. I wasn't quite run into the ground from following her, but it was a near thing. I caught my breath as subtle as I could, no wheezing, no pressing my hand against my side where a stitch sent sharp hurting into me with every step. Looking around was a good distraction.

We kept going—we passed little house after little house and stopped at none of them. They were getting a little more space in between them instead of being right on top of each other, sharing walls. The more we walked, the more I expected Dell to turn, to duck through one of the low doors. The fog turned to mist and clung to my skin, made me chill to the bone, clammy.

I told myself I'd been concentrating on that and that's why I didn't see the house at the end of the row, the way it rose up all of a sudden like a magic cottage in some fairytale. It was pretty much the same as all the others—no windows and the door held open for folks to come and go. But it was a little bit bigger, and a chimney was pumping smoke out, signaling a busy fire inside.

The house across the little street from it was the only one I'd seen with a closed door. The door was blue. But I didn't give it too much attention because the smoke coming from the bigger house didn't smell like pine logs. The scent wasn't nearly as green. And when we got close to the open door, the aroma of bread just about knocked me over.

My stomach clenched and rumbled, but I settled with myself not to ask—I had my pride.

Dell led me to the open door—and my pride got ready to take a beating. We walked into the house, full of the smell of fresh bread and it was like sitting by the oven, warm and delicious, even though I was only on the threshold of this house. It might have been that I was hungry; it might have been that it was the best bread in the entire world. I would have put even odds on both.

My chest hurt and my fingers jerked, and I ignored them so I could focus on the smell, on drawing it in. Something in my middle twanged like an over-plucked rubber band, and I followed Dell over the door saddle and into whatever was going to happen—because surely something was.

Speculation. I didn't know enough, didn't know what signs to read. There had to be something that would let me know what kind of place this was—I just had to know where to look.

The inside of the house wasn't as dark as I'd have expected, if I'd stopped to think about it before going inside. There were lamps lit everywhere. It wasn't Marty's kitchen, but the scents wafting out of it—more than just that amazing bread now that I was inside and could smell everything—were similar to those coming from Marty's stove, good cooked meat of some kind and vegetables.

And the woman at the stove, white apron and all, might as well have been Marty. I felt disloyal for the thought—no one was just like Marty. But if someone was going to be *like* Marty, this stranger was a good candidate for it. Her hands were small and agile, her back bent but strong as she lifted a metal pan of something mouthwatering out of the oven to stir its juices around, basting the large chunk of marbled meat in the middle. And her face, when she turned to see who was intruding, split into the same kind of smile Marty had always worn for Ben and me when she was glad to see us.

It hurt, worse than the stitch still stabbing into my side, deep and cold, how much I missed her. I was surviving, just like she had asked of me, because there wasn't anything else I could do—but she hadn't told me it'd be a lonely business, and I sure hadn't known until the thick of the woods.

"Who's your friend, Dell?" The voice, at least, was different. Nothing like Marty, an accent like no one else's in town making her consonants harsh and blurry.

Dell moved further into the kitchen, wrapped an arm around the old woman's waist. "I found her in the woods, and she followed me home. Her name's Hank, Granny. Can I keep her?"

It was more than she'd said to me on our entire trek. I tried not to feel bitter about that, but wasn't sure how successful I was, since I had to bite my lip and look at the ground past my clenched fists. Dell wasn't whispering now—wasn't loud either, but she had the same easy way about her that everyone else coming and going in their houses had, like this was a totally normal evening.

Nothing about this was normal to me—certainly not the way I noticed her voice and how her consonants didn't do the same thing as the woman she called 'granny.' I'd never been real good at propriety, true, but this was some kind of inappropriate. Dell had a pretty way of talking now that she wasn't being as quiet as she had been, and I took notice enough that I managed to look up and make half a second of eye contact.

"Ain't I got something to say in whether or not you keep me?" It might have sounded like a small cup of sass if I'd been in a better humor and if my stomach hadn't chosen just then to cramp up so hard I almost doubled over. Or, I realized with creeping dread, not my stomach. My damn uterus.

I was starting my flow right in the middle of this stranger's kitchen, while I was thinking about flirting with the girl who'd saved me from the woods where I was living rough. I had completely forgotten—I hadn't packed any of my pads or anything to make me feel better. I spared a curse for Marty for that.

The laugh fighting its way out of my throat just about choked me, but I held it in, hard enough that I had another coughing fit. They were going to think I have tuberculosis at this rate. "I'm not sick—I just thought of something funny." Not the best explanation, much less the best introduction, nothing smooth that would make them trust me. At least it was honest—honesty seemed to have worked out real well on Dell.

She eyed me, tilted her head and waited for a sharp-tongued response that I didn't have in me to find and give to her. After an awkward minute, she moved to a cabinet, retrieved a glass. Filled it with water from the pitcher on the counter. When Dell offered it to me, she held onto it, held against the pressure of my fingers when I tried to take it from her. "You can call her Granny."

The old woman leaned against her counter, chuckled behind Dell's back. Dell blushed fit to beat the band—Marty had always said that, and I had no idea what it even meant. And I had no idea what was making Dell turn red like that. But I was lightheaded from hunger and running after her to get here, and my cramps were twisting my whole midsection into a hard knot tied around how empty my belly was. And everything just seemed funnier. I had to slap a hand over my mouth to keep from giggling at the pink of Dell's cheeks.

If Dell were telling me just to call the old woman Granny, that meant it was more name than relation probably. Granny probably had other names Dell called her, but they both had better sense than I'd shown about personal power. I flinched back a little, all laughter dropped out of my mouth, when Granny moved around Dell to come close and brush my filthy hair, which had dried in even worse knots than before, away from my cheek. Her fingers were steady and her practical nails were short but sharp when they grazed my ear.

"Dell." Granny kept her eyes on mine, watched as I pulled more of my serious up over all the humor. "Dell, show Hank where the necessaries are and put her in the top room." She patted my shoulder and left the kitchen without another word or any sort of fanfare. I stood where she'd left me, mouth agape and jaw slack. Which didn't stop me from hoping that the necessaries Granny had mentioned included some kind of pads.

There was something complicated shaping Dell's mouth. Her lips were red like she'd been sucking on fruit, but I'd been with her the whole walk home and she hadn't done anything of the sort. She was nearly smiling.

"Come on, Hank. We'll get you settled." She put that glass of water on the counter and then moved to touch the same shoulder that Granny had patted, a weirder echo of a strange reassurance.

It seemed like they really were setting up to keep me. I'd have to talk to Granny more, get a feel for the place, figure out how I could earn my way. But I'd also heard a couple rumors I was just starting to put together—about people in the woods who got their mail delivered in town, but there was no P. O. box number next to the slot that held that mystery mail—so I couldn't count my lucky stars and relax just yet. The stars didn't seem like they'd been lucky for any in my family, honestly—or for anyone who wasn't a Reborn.

Even without luck, though, I didn't have a lot of choice—and with blood soaking into my underwear, I wanted to believe in the offer. I followed Dell, and she opened a door I had taken for a closet. Beyond it, the stairs led to some kind of cellar. There was no way I was far enough north for a cellar to be easy to dig—the only time anyone in Wanton attempted that, they'd hit milky green groundwater about four feet down.

The stairs went deep though, no mistake about that. And Dell headed down them without any kind of hesitation. I wasn't going to let her see me afraid—I wasn't a baby, after all—so I started after her again, making a habit out of keeping in her footsteps. The first step creaked under my weight, but she didn't even look back up to make sure it held me. I winced just the same. I had to be heavier than her, so I didn't much trust the steps just because she went first.

It wasn't even a very tall set of steps—just enough that we didn't bump our heads on the ceiling beams that were actually the floor beams of the kitchen above us. It wasn't a room proper that we landed in though; it was more like a long, dark hallway.

It was a damn tunnel. Somehow they'd dug a shallow tunnel and kept it from flooding. The floor was stone under my feet, and where would that have even come from? They'd have had to cart it in from somewhere north; we didn't have that kind of rock.

The tunnel held on to the coldness of the air upstairs and the walls—packed dirt, it looked like—just about radiated it. I shivered, wrapped my arms around my middle and held on to my opposite elbows. The cold must have felt magical when it was hot outside. All it did was unnerve me when everything else hadn't been able to make me entirely worried. Something about it made me want to lay down and turn my belly up, bare my throat, show that I wasn't a threat.

The hall was long—and the shadows were strange in it. It seemed bigger than the house upstairs, at least from what I'd seen of the kitchen.

But Dell wasn't pausing, so at least I didn't have to fight that much against the instinct. She strode down the hall, her shoes louder on the stone than they were on the wood floor upstairs, with the confidence of someone who knew where they were going. It was reassuring. Until she opened another door at the end of the hall. More stairs. I stopped, my foot on the bottom run, feeling like I was in a movie or a novel or something, about to take a step I couldn't go back from. I looked behind me down the hall; with the door we'd come in closed, it was lit only by a light burning halfway down the hall, a bare bulb in a wire cage.

This stairway felt like we were somewhere else, somewhere secret. And that was the whole point of a tunnel, wasn't it? To make a secret path somewhere? It would have been a whole lot of effort to just not want to go outside. Though it would make things convenient—no danger from Reborn and you could go from place to place in the dead of night if you wanted to. Maybe all the houses were connected this way. But there was that fence—I doubted the Reborn ever made it into this weird hidden town, so there wasn't much need for being able to avoid them this way.

These stairs creaked even louder than the first set. Weren't used that often. There wasn't any dust or anything, but they weren't worn in the middle of the step from feet trudging up and down. And if they were so loud, they couldn't actually be much of a secret.

But maybe I was also just missing some kind of trick to walking on them; not a single stair let out a groan as Dell climbed up. The wood kept her secrets. And when we reached the top of the staircase, higher than the one we'd come down, Dell knocked. It sounded like a pattern, complicated and rhythmic.

That made sense for a secret passage—why not a secret knock, while they were at it? I was too tired to do anything more than not have any expectations. I was too worn out for predicting what was to happen next. Even so, my heart fluttered when the door opened wide and a boy who looked almost just like my brother Ben held it for us to pass. For half a minute, my lungs clenched and all my air rushed out of my mouth, and I thought it really was Ben, somehow escaped from James's big blue car, somehow made it all the way back down the road to find the trail I'd forged. But the boy grinned with no hint of recognition, a friendly stranger, and my heart slowed back down with enough disappointment to hunch my shoulders. Not Ben, not Ben, not Ben, it beat at me until I managed to catch my breath and offer my hand.

"You can call me Hank." Everyone was going to know my true name at this rate. I should have told them to call me Henry. It was my daddy's name, or so Ben had reminded me when he was irritated with me, calling me Henrietta like that was going to make me mind my manners. It had never seemed the right shape for me, my hips already too wide for it, stretching it out and then getting it tangled in my hair. I wouldn't be able to make it work—not with Granny and Dell already calling me Hank—but maybe I could fix it in my own head. This boy that wasn't Ben could call me Hank, and I'd be Henry to myself, and that'd give me breathing room.

Dell cleared her throat, and I realized I'd just been standing there, swaying. The boy still held the door so we could step into a room that, near as I could see just looking around, didn't have any windows nor doors, no other way out than the way we'd come in.

The boy that wasn't Ben stepped aside just far enough not to touch me, shoved Dell with a playful shoulder—that really did just about break my heart; Ben had pulled the same move on me more times than I'd be able to count. "It's real nice to meet you, Hank. You can call me Jimmy."

It was just as well he was a Jimmy—he didn't seem to have enough sour in that smile to be a Jim. And if he was actually a James, well, I didn't want to think about that name much more than I had to. It wouldn't have done him any favors with me at this point. Didn't much matter—he had no reason to tell me his full name, not any more than I'd have had to tell him Henrietta.

The more I looked, the less he looked like Ben anyway. His hair was blonder, almost gold. And Jimmy was taller than me but probably shorter than Ben. His jeans rode low on his hips, and he'd foregone a shirt. Jimmy scratched at a bug bite high on one shoulder while I looked him over—Dell rolled her eyes at him and then gestured over at a ladder propped up in the corner.

At least, I'd registered it as being propped up. When I looked closer, the ladder was secured to the wall right at the top, and there was a trap door up there. Dell nudged my arm, pushed me along with her fingers on the swell of meat above my elbow until we were at the base. "Granny wanted me to put you in the top room. That one's my favorite."

She climbed the ladder ahead of me though she looked down to make sure I was still following even without her physically steering me around. I looked from her to Jimmy and then back to her—and then at Jimmy again. I wanted to ask them what the hell kind of house this was, and did they know it didn't make any damn sense? But that seemed rude, even in my exhausted daze. All things considered, I probably ought not be so blunt. Instead, I hauled myself up and then right on through the trap door after she'd gone through it.

The top room, as she and Granny had called it, was a little round space with a piece on one edge shaved off. I'd have figured it for some kind of tower room, but I hadn't noticed any actual towers on my way in through town. And it had nary a window, so it matched every other place I'd seen in that regard.

That was just details, though. Mostly, it felt comfortable. It was lit with three lights, lanterns, really, one on each bedside table and one on the dresser. The tables flanked a big, wide bed.

That bed looked unearthly soft and clean and I was aware, with a rush of further self-consciousness, of how dirty I was even if I hadn't bled through my pants yet. I had to stink. And all of a sudden, I did smell myself, my ripeness rushing up into my nostrils: dirt, sweat, hunger, fear, and the final insult of blood.

Either Dell was just being polite—maybe she was practicing her manners—or she nursed more than a little pity for me. She pointed her two fingers held together over toward the flat part of the wall where there was a little door, painted white. It didn't have a frame and blended in with the wall—how they knew where to look when they needed to slam something, I had no idea. "Go on. The bathroom's in there. You'll find everything you need under the sink."

She didn't make any move to usher me over there—leaving me to my privacy and what was left of the shreds of my dignity. Going to the bathroom in the woods hadn't really bothered me even though it was never going to be my favorite thing. I'd surprised myself by being pretty pleased with the reality of camping out, outside of the constant danger and worry. But a real bathroom? There was no way I was passing that up.

I stuttered out my gratitude and made a beeline for that little white door. It shut behind me with a solid click; it felt secure and if nothing else, I'd know if anyone tried to come in after me. With that figured out, I turned around to get a good look—and my knees just about gave out. Every surface was so clean. There was a real stand-up shower. We'd never had one. Ours had been a tub with a hand-held sprayer, and we counted ourselves lucky to have good enough water pressure for that. There were neighbors between us and town who bathed in a tub in their yard with well water regardless of the temperature outside.

The shower piping was hooked up to a big claw foot tub, cast iron. Heavy as sin, had to be, even empty. But it was up in this weird room, and I'd figure out what that meant about my situation later on. In the meantime, there was an awful lot of white tile to take in, a white counter, and a bright white light over the sink.

They had a generator somewhere, the light bulb in the tunnel had told me that. And it put out enough juice that they had lights in their bathrooms, electric lights. But the bedroom lamps were oil. The house was already weird enough by design, and I didn't understand how it could rightfully exist. I wasn't about to complain though—not with all this clean and pretty sitting there waiting for me to take advantage of it so I could be clean, too.

She'd said under the sink so I crouched down and opened the cabinet door; it didn't even squeak. There was a stash of cloth pads in the back, clean and tidy. Marty and I had sewn a bunch of them the summer I was twelve, when I'd had my first monthly, as she tended to call it. I'd been grossed out, the feeling of something sliding out of my body just too strange. It wasn't gross, she'd told me. It was where life came from. I told her that sometimes life was just gross. And painful— because another cramp knotted me right up until I had to hold on to the thin wooden cabinet door.

When the cramp passed, I stood carefully and checked the bathroom door again. It had a lock, and I turned it, locked myself in so

I could strip out of my clothes. I left them in a heap on the floor, reluctant to touch them enough to fold them. Then I leaned back down to snag my underpants. They needed a wash, and I could do that here and now. The shower pipes were copper and gleaming, and there was soap and a washcloth in the white, white, white tub.

The water didn't turn purely hot but after my chill in the tunnel, it was warm enough. And there was a lot of it all rushing down. I stepped into the shower like it was the nicest place I'd ever been in my whole life and drew the curtain around me with a flourish. The soap even smelled good, something a little spicy. I used it to wash my underpants, then wrung them out and hung them to dry over the shower rod; I washed my body in my routine order and marveled at how clear my skin looked without a film of sweat and dust leaving me grimy.

Sand got everywhere; there was no way to avoid it—another reason to feel lucky we didn't get many dusters. The whole damn state would blow away if all the sand took to the wind at the same time.

I scrubbed and scrubbed, barely even controlling my body. I watched my hands move, wearing my mother's ring, saw my skin covered in soap as I lathered it with the washrag until I felt raw and new. My face burned, and it was only when I remembered that I really was alone, that I was the only one making any noises, that I realized the sobbing sounds tore from me. I washed my face with more soap and the washcloth, hiding my eyes until I was all cried out and my eyes hurt from having run out of tears.

Crying was stupid. By the time I stopped my babying, rinsed myself off, and turned the taps off, I was all over ashamed of myself. Weeping never helped anyone do anything, even if I'd needed it after everything I'd lived through only to wind up here. I couldn't deny that I felt better, cleaner inside and out, but that pressure inside me kept me alive. Now it was mostly gone, except for just a little bit that lingered and gave me a headache.

The headache might also be chalked up to hunger—I resolved to towel myself off and find my way back to that kitchen. In for a damn penny—if I was going to use up their hospitality then I needed to be practical and ask for a sandwich or some scrap of something. I leaned out of the curtain to grab for a couple of clean folded towels in a stack on the back of the toilet. One for my hair and one for my body, arms and legs and middle and back. There was a clean pair of underwear in my bag, at least. Between that and the homemade pad, I felt very nearly human even before I hiked my dirty jeans back on, then topped them with one of my old t-shirts.

I was ready to face people again. And to do that, I needed to move. I took a deep breath and unlocked the door. My hair was going to dry like a rat's nest, but I'd brush it out later. Hunger trumped looks hands down.

While I'd been in the shower, someone had been in the room. The bed was turned down, all inviting and cozy, showing off its soft, sleepy sheets like a girl flashing her ankle. And there was a tray—a tray with a bowl full of some kind of stew, steam steady rising off it.

The surprise of it held me stock still on the threshold like I was a dog and someone had told me to stay. Food delivered, unasked for when I had been preparing myself to beg, just like that. Food and another glass of that clean water like they had it to spare even after my long shower.

If my eyes hadn't already smarted from crying—not to mention my pride—I'd have teared up again. Instead, I fell to, ate with my fingers and used the crusty bread to sop up mouthfuls, scoop mouthfuls up, really, risking a burn to my tongue.

I couldn't identify the meat by flavor, but I didn't have a single care to spare for that. It was kind of like pork, which we'd had a decent amount of growing up, but it felt like beef between my teeth. We hadn't had much of that; cows were too precious to eat. All of my own food, before it had run out, had been cold and simple whether it was fruit or cheese or out of a can. And the water—there was an ice cube in it. An ice cube meant they had a freezer somewhere and didn't mind letting me know about it. It was just one ice cube so they weren't really showing off, but I was impressed even so. I fished it out with my fingers and let it melt on my tongue, freezing my lips and my cheeks.

There had to be some work or something I could do to pay them back. I'd figure it out, but I didn't want to be so deep in their debt. In the meantime, the message of the turned-down bed was plenty loud and clear for me to understand. Once I'd finished licking my fingers clean, the bed was the most irresistible thing I'd ever seen; I shucked the jeans and climbed in under the covers.

The last time I'd taken a nap in the middle of the day, I'd had chicken pox—I'd been thirteen, caught it late. The itchy red spots ran from stern to aft. With the fever that came with them, I'd imagined chickens pecking all over me all night long—I'd screamed from it in my sleep and Marty had come running to wake me up. So had Ben. Between the two of them—Marty held on to my feet and Ben to my shoulders—they'd shook me until I woke up from my nightmare. Ben's face was the first face I'd seen, and I'd known that as long as I did, the giant chickens with their needle beaks couldn't get me.

When I told him that, Ben had slept on my floor in a bundle of blankets and pillows. He'd stayed until my fever broke—and with my fever went the dreams.

We'd shared eggs for breakfast and laughed over my nightmares, though I'd sounded darn feeble compared to their hearty sounds of amusement. I'd been safe though, with food in my mouth and the impatience that came with feeling better as one recovered from a serious illness. Marty had brushed through my hair, had picked through the tangles until the brush could stroke through.

I'd fallen back asleep and skipped dreaming altogether. And something here felt the same, even with the secret path to reach it and all that had happened since Seymour arrived to make up a different kind of distance, felt safe until I could at least close my eyes. I didn't notice when I fell asleep and I didn't have any dreams at all, at least none that I could recall. Trading dreams for a favor was a shady business anyway. Instead, the bed told me I was cared for, no matter what I had to trade—it felt like someone was looking out for me even though I didn't believe in any god.

CHAPTER ELEVEN

Hospitality Is A Debt

I 'd fallen asleep with such a good feeling that when I woke up, in the dark and the warm still air all around me, I actually expected to be back in my room at Marty's, the intervening days and betrayals nothing but my imagination taking a nasty turn. But my bed had been firmer than this one, the frame creakier when I turned and tossed in my sleep. Here, I rolled over and there was nary a sound but my own thoughts, my own inner conviction that a little bit more sleep would be a very fine thing indeed.

That was a point and a very good one at that. But the softness of the mattress had made my back tight after a week of sleeping on the ground, and even as I stretched my toes out as far as I could, I knew I had to get up or I'd drift off for hours and then regret it when I woke up like a big knot of rope that had gotten soaked and then dried out in the sun.

The bedside lantern had been turned down—someone, maybe the same someone who had brought the food when I was in the shower, had taken care of that and retrieved my dirty dishes, all without me stirring a single hair. Seemed like I was closer to unconscious than to plain old asleep if I was looking to be honest. I sighed, and leaned over enough to twist the little knob on the lantern, cranked the wick up enough to brighten the flame.

The extra little light was enough to reveal a pertinent bit of information—namely, whoever had been in there had also taken the dirty clothes I'd left in a pile beside the bed. My jeans were gone, and in their place was a dress. A clean dress, spread out on a chair. It looked to be about my size, but it was still a dress; I never wore the things.

Especially not on Sundays. After our morning chores, me and Ben were allowed to do pretty much whatever we wanted on Sundays. That usually involved fishing and water and mud and coming home covered in sand burrs.

Still, the dress was clean, and that was the highest praise I had for anything at this point. I tugged it down over my head—my hair was mostly dry though I'd left behind a damp pillow when I sat up—and into place over my frame. It fit pretty well, though the top was a little big and the ass was going to be a little tight when I sat down. But it was all sorts of old-fashioned, with a square neck that meant the extra fabric on top didn't even point down to anything interesting. It just sat there and didn't leave me exposed or uncomfortable or anything else that would warrant a complaint or justify me not wearing the thing.

The fabric was a faded cotton, plain blue worn paler in some spots, with short sleeves and a dropped waist. That was the part that was tight on my butt then. The skirt's hem at least hit my knees, and I wondered, without spending too much time dissecting, what Dell might think of how I looked in it.

Most likely, ridiculous actually. I shifted my posture, put my feet closer, and reminded myself: when you sit, make sure your knees are together like a lady. Jenny (and how long had it been since I'd thought of her?) had always sat prim and upright; it was one of the things I'd noticed straight off about her. If I could manage to just act like she did, maybe I could make the whole dress thing work.

That feeling of wellbeing lasted just about until I reached for the handle on the trap door. I froze for a second, right before my hand gripped the latch. I should have tested it earlier. As soon as I'd been alone in the room, Dell and Jimmy disappeared, off doing whatever it was they did in this fenced-in town. But I'd needed to get clean, and I'd needed to eat and sleep. I wouldn't have been in any state to fight my way free anyway.

I took a deep breath and hauled on the trapdoor. Nothing, not even a little bit of give. I was just as stuck as I thought I'd be—probably more because the more I yanked on that handle, the more I realized I couldn't hear much of anything. I banged on the door until my fist was sore, and then I switched hands so I could bang some more.

But for all the ruckus I kicked up, there wasn't even a hint that it made it to anyone else's ears. The trap door didn't so much as rattle in its frame. There could be a baby sleeping down in that little anteroom for all the disruption my fuss probably caused.

I hadn't seen any other doors or windows at all in the bathroom. But I double checked just in case. I could toss things about the room, but for some reason, I wasn't feeling that level of panic. I wasn't feeling that level of pissed off either. Yeah, I was locked in against my will, but they didn't know me. I was a stranger, and they'd just taken me in. Breaking things seemed like ill treatment in the face of that, even with being locked in. And the things in this little prison room were beautiful. It seemed kind of tragic to be considering breaking them into pieces just because I had been too hungry-stupid and tired-numb to sense a trap behind the trap door.

If they meant me harm, they probably wouldn't have bothered with all the good treatment either. That sort of effort wouldn't have made much sense. I flopped back down onto the bed and closed my eyes to think it through and get my bearings.

It couldn't have been fifteen minutes before there was the soft sound of a bell. Then there was a long pause before the trap door lifted up with a gentle creak that had me scrambling around to the far side of the bed to put a little distance between myself and my visitor.

Jimmy stuck his head up far enough to look around, grinned when he saw me against the wall. "You decent?"

My heart picked up pace—and it didn't slow down just because, as near as I could tell, there weren't any good reason. I leaned forward against the bed before my knees gave out and sent me crashing to the floor. Never knew who was below us, that kind of noise—if they could hear it any better with the trap door ajar—was always rude.

Jimmy opened the door wider until it slammed onto the floor behind him, hitched himself the rest of the way up, concern etched in his eyebrows and his outstretched hand. He didn't move fast, kept it slow and easy. "Hey, I didn't mean to startle you—Granny figured she ought to talk to you now that you've had a chance to clean up and eat and sleep."

He left the bed between us, smart enough to give me room not to panic, to pick my dignity back up and fix it where I needed it.

"Sorry. Wasn't expecting anybody." I muttered it into the bed cover, and mostly meant it. That was about as polite as I could stand to be at the moment, my face hot and my skin too tight. I knew I'd be red and it wouldn't be from the sun.

"Don't worry about it. You've been sleeping rough, I bet." Jimmy's smile was lopsided. "Takes a while to adjust again, don't it?" His expression stayed steady and nonthreatening—I saw it from the corner of my eye. There was something not quite right about that, but I couldn't tell what it was and there were other things to consider. I gave him my profile for a minute until I felt a little stronger, a little more in control of my own body.

One of his eyes drooped a little. I hadn't noticed it earlier, too caught up thinking he looked like Ben, too tangled up in wanting him to be Ben to see many of his own details beyond a rough sketch. Actually looking at him, seeing him again, there was even less resemblance. He was just a boy. Well, hell. Not just a boy—really more of a man in the same way Ben was. But that was the bulk of the sameness there.

I'd already noticed his lighter hair, how he was shorter than Ben. But Jimmy was broader, probably stronger. His thick hair was messy and the color matched the freckles on his nose. It was his right eye that drooped, and that was the side his smile was lopsided on, too. And he obviously knew about being nervous of strangers with the way he still didn't come any closer, how he just let me stand up on my own. I watched him, still taking in all the details I could, down to the yellow stitching on his jeans. Not quite Seeing. But close enough for horseshoes, probably.

"Hank?" Jimmy rubbed at his left eye with the heel of his hand. "You keep looking at me funny like that, and I'm going to start in on sneezing and I'd rather not." He turned his back on me, heading for the door. "You come on downstairs when you're ready, and Granny'll be waiting. Just knock like this." And he demonstrated a rhythmic knock, seven beats long, on the floor—before he dropped through the opening like he didn't even need the ladder. Then he was gone, door left open behind him and I could hear his whistling until he was gone from the room below, too.

Well. Well, hell. I dried my sweaty scared palm on the hem of my dress. My borrowed dress. The dress I wore because someone had stolen my real clothes. I walked soft over to the trap door and stared down at the ladder for a minute before I reached my foot out and headed down.

It was draftier in a dress, that was one thing. Another was the way my thighs rubbed together. And I was more aware than I'd have figured on being that anyone who stood below me would get an eyeful straight up my skirt. I tried not to let that shake me even though it made me want to clamp my knees together, skirt fabric tight and bunched between them.

Instead of doing that, I hopped down when I was still three rungs above the floor. The impact made my ankles sting a little, but even that was welcome—it made me feel more awake, more aware than I'd been climbing down. Since climbing up in the first place, even. It wasn't like I'd been in a trance or hypnotized really, but I'd been unsettled and off my guard, shaken up by dirt and soap and soft sheets. I needed to talk to Granny, to find out what they wanted from me. I could barter work; I was strong.

I kept up cataloging my skills on the walk back to the kitchen. It was a surprise that none of it felt strange anymore—I'd been this way only once, and now it felt just as natural as anything. I imitated the knock that Jimmy had shown me, and the door opened, didn't even creak. The smell of fresh bread once again nearly pulled me in by my ears.

"Come and sit yourself down." Granny had a different sort of voice from Marty, but I wanted to mind her just the same. Realizing it made me stubborn; I stood where I was and looked a long solid look at her.

She just looked back at me, waited with a pursed mouth and her hands wrapped up in her apron until I couldn't stand not doing what I was told anymore. I stepped far enough into the kitchen to snag a chair at the table and sit like I was visiting for Sunday dinner. Granny nodded at me then, a sharp jerk of her head that looked like approval.

Marty had taught me some manners, at least, and it hit me that I hadn't given them a single grateful word. "Thank you." Even though it hurt coming out of my mouth, I didn't give myself any choice. "The meal and the bath and the…" I wasn't sure what to say about the dress. I wanted my own clothes back, dammit. But it belonged to someone and lending it to me, a stranger, meant whoever that someone was, they were doing without. "Thank you for the clothing, too, though I don't mind my own at all." At least I'd gotten that out there without choking on my own audacity.

"Hank." The way it came out of her mouth made my back straighten right up like there was a ruler strapped to it. My name fit too easy in her mouth—she'd laid it out before I even got to the table. "Welcome to my house." It was formal, like she invoked something, and she might as well have.

Guests were troublesome things, Marty always said. She didn't have guests, she had visitors, like James who stayed a bit and left before nightfall. Or like Seymour who paid for the privilege out in our fields. Any longer than that, any more than that, and you had to start taking care of folks, look out for their safety, keep them fed and watered and locked up safe and tight at night. You had to be hospitable. There were rules about that sort of thing: if someone suffered under your roof, got hurt bad or dead or Reborn, that was a mark against you, meant you and your hospitality couldn't be trusted. Better not to risk it, she'd lectured us when we'd wanted our friends to stay over or when the occasional wanderer had worked in our barn for a day before she'd sent them on with a sack of food but no shelter.

"I appreciate your hospitality." I said it clear and straight out, my part of the invocation. "If there's anything I can do, something to repay it, I'll do it." I didn't want to offer more than my work, but letting Granny set the task was the right thing to do, the only way to do things given how Marty had raised me. She'd have spanked me clear across the backfield if I'd responded with anything different.

Seemed like Granny was of a similar mind because she finally smiled at my words, gave me a friendlier look instead of the kind someone would bestow on a freeloader. "As it happens, there is something. But we won't worry at it yet. First, I want to know how you happened around here."

It would be better to keep my starting point a secret, otherwise I'd give up Marty and everything that had happened, and I wanted to protect her still. But there weren't a lot of towns around either. So I wouldn't start at the very beginning. "I was in the woods for about a week. Dell found me at the edge of the river, drinking water." Vague but true. I wasn't going to lie to someone giving me shelter.

"You came from somewhere before that, make no mistake." Granny was sharp, and her mouth made it clear she knew I was hiding—and to what purpose. "I won't push on that though, you keep those secrets in your pocket until you're ready to tell me. In the meantime, you'll stay here, in that room. Whatever you're running from, it isn't likely to wind up here."

She didn't know that, there was no way to know that. It didn't seem likely that James would know the woods or know how to make it back into them; his soft hands and clean pants weren't suited for this kind of terrain. But it hadn't seemed likely that Ben would be carted off by city cousins for some of their experiments either, so what did I know? There was only so much disbelief I could suspend if I wanted to stay on my guard, be ready for things to shift and change again. That seemed to be what it took to stay alive.

Still, that fence was a mighty convincing argument all on its own. And the guards with their guns didn't hurt either.

"You can't promise that, can't say they won't show up here." It was gruffer than I meant it to come out. But it was still what I needed to say. "Can't make any such claim." Marty had lied to me, I knew that much. And if Marty could lie, some strange old woman in the middle of a kitchen in a town that didn't have a lick of business even existing could lie to me, too.

Her salt-and-pepper head tilted to one side as she looked at me, the way a dog would look at me if I were doing something funny that it was trying to understand. Though I bet Granny understood a lot more than any dog, old or new. "Don't expect you to just believe. Telling you to stay anyway. It's the right thing to do, and you'll be useful around here. Unless you think the woods'll be friendlier?"

They wouldn't be. I was out of food and luck with no hope of finding my own way, if I'd even had a plan for where I was going anymore. Marty's advice hadn't been good advice, but should I risk heading further north, running into my cousin? I shook my head, afraid of what might come out of my mouth in that instant, what kind of crazy confessions about the Reborn I'd seen and the shadows and my dreams might come spilling out for Granny to eat up.

I caught my breath. Bit my lip until I could speak again without worrying what my tongue would say given half a chance. "I appreciate the offer, and I'll take you up on it if you think I really can be useful around here for you."

"Not much of an offer, really—other option would be to turn you out. You'd be prey in a day, day and a half, I reckon." Granny's eyes weren't so kind on that note, had a flinty grey behind the blue that sparked up against the side of my little bit of pride recovering from the indignity of being charity.

As unsettling and upsetting as it was, I gave in to the idea of it, pictured myself wandering the woods, getting weaker, colder, smaller as the days passed until no one would even know it had been me once upon a time if a Reborn—when a Reborn—finally found me. I remembered those finger bones and looked at my own hands, imagined touching things without any of my skin or my nails or my flesh.

"I don't know about that, ma'am. But I do appreciate that you ain't making me take that chance." In truth, it didn't matter if I'd been prey in a week or two weeks or two years—without some sort of shelter, I'd be caught eventually and probably starve to death in the meantime. If I was caught, it'd be like that squirrel or a chubby bird in winter. Lying to myself about it wasn't going to get me anything better than dead or worse.

"Long as you know it." Granny nodded the way she had when I'd taken a seat at the kitchen table, firm and proud. She had some authority over me now; we both knew it, cemented as surely as if we'd shaken hands on the deal. "Now, if you're interested in getting to work, I've got some animals need tending. Just inside the fence—we don't truck with going outside it much; our job's in here."

She'd thrown it out like bait, as wriggly a worm as I'd ever threaded on a hook. "Your job?" Like it was the whole town working on one project.

"That's what I said. You don't pay it any mind right now." Her tone was satisfied, like I'd done what she figured I'd do—that rankled. I didn't want to be so easily predictable to her, but I didn't know enough to do anything else. And if I was easy to figure out, if I was an easy face to read? Well, that was that, and it was better to be a thrifty honest woman than a lucrative liar, as Marty had always said.

Though I wasn't entirely sure how that applied at the moment.

"I still do appreciate it. Though I'm curious, I can tell you that." I could be charming. At least, I figured I could try. Ben had always laughed at my sass.

Granny just snorted, an inelegant sound from her long nose. "Curiosity killed the cat, and satisfaction brought him back—I doubt you'd appreciate either state of being though." But she followed it up with enough of a laugh and joined me at the table, finally. "You ever take care of chickens? I've got a good dozen, we like them for the eggs. They never have taken to Dell, she can't go in the pen without coming out henpecked."

Having something I knew so well laid out before me like a dinner made my eyes close and breath all rush out despite the suspicions I was trying to hold on to. I was getting more practice at dealing with surprises, so I didn't jump up and cry. "I looked after our chickens back home. Do you have just a pen or you got a coop, too?" If Dell wasn't having good luck with the chickens, then the coop probably needed cleaning.

We fell into an easy rhythm of questions and answers and by the time she pointed me at the door, I was feeling more confident. That stopped when she called me back for one more thing. "I'll tell you just the once—you try to go outside the fence, and they'll shoot you. Won't care who you are or what your name is. You don't have the right permissions, and you'd be bringing it on yourself. The coop's around the back of the house with the blue door. That door's locked, by the way."

There didn't really seem to be any kind of adequate response to that. No wonder she didn't seem worried about the Reborn getting in. Dell must have had some kind of free range permit or something. Though it made those guards who'd quizzed me at the gate seem more frightening in hindsight. If they were really so eager to use those guns, I had been in more danger than Dell had let on.

"I'll be careful. And I'll be seeing to that coop right now if you've got my clothes handy." There was no way I was doing farm chores in a dress, especially one that didn't even belong to me.

Granny shook her head. "Go on and wear that old thing. You won't hurt it none." It was like she had heard me thinking and decided I needed a lesson.

It also seemed like every time I asked after my clothes, she hadn't wanted to give me an answer. Or my clothes. Her tone didn't leave any open windows for my concerns about mess to climb through but I tried. "Cleaning's a dirty job—are there any pants I can wear?" My legs felt exposed enough just sitting in the kitchen. And Dell had been wearing pants, so I knew it wasn't something about me being a girl.

But Granny just waved her hand, absentminded like I was going to fall for that, and turned her attention to a bowl of peas in their pods on the table. Her fingers were nimble as she shelled some, snapped some. The fresh green smell of the hulls made my mouth water. Without looking, Granny offered me a raw pea. "You're hungry, there's always food. No need to be stingy with it."

I hesitated, but my mouth already watered. I trembled a little when I reached out, careful not to brush her hand with my fingers. Seemed rude somehow, or flat out dangerous. She didn't look a thing like it, but I had a sudden sense, a knot in my gut that might have been a cramp except for how high up it was, that she'd be able to grab me—and if she did, I wouldn't get loose until she turned me loose.

That probably wouldn't end well. Marty had taken chickens who'd stopped laying and wrung their necks; I'd always watched from a distance because I worked with them too close every day to feel any good about it. Then Marty would pluck each chicken and boil them until their meat fell off the bones, until she could just pick it all to pieces with her hands even though it was still steaming hot. I got the feeling, looking at the steady way Granny held that pea out, she'd do the same to me if I gave her an excuse for it.

I took the treat from her and nothing happened. I brought it to my mouth, crunched into it, pod and all. The moisture in it was sweet, clean. It tasted like raw dirt and sunshine. I dropped my eyes, ashamed now that I'd been afraid of her, then mumbled my thanks and exited through the door she'd pointed at. I'd ask after my clothes again later.

Even with that thought, my feet paused on the threshold, and I looked back. Granny was still messing with the peas. Stuck inside the fence, that much was crystal clear and not comfortable at all, the rest of it felt... familiar. Close to hundreds of other days when I'd woken up and done my chores while Marty fixed us something to eat. My heart worried that once I stepped outside, everything inside would change. I worried that once I left, I was never going to be able to go back to that simple kitchen. It was foolish—I'd only spent a few hours there. It wasn't home, their hospitality aside, and it was probably better it not start feeling that way.

With another deep breath, I finally made it out onto the path by the front door. I was alone—I'd been alone since Marty turned me out. I hated to think of it that way, it felt rebellious and ungrateful, but it was more honest than saying I'd left of my own will, no matter that Marty had made me choose it. This was different—I heard voices and people bustling about in their houses, coming and going. None of them close enough I'd have to talk to them, but they'd hear me if I hollered.

I didn't holler. I followed Granny's instructions back around the other side of the house with the blue door—and didn't stop to test the lock.

The coop was bigger than I'd expected. The wire came up and met in an arch, tied together with sharp glints of razor wire, a good two feet over my head. Maybe their chickens were more interested in practicing flying or maybe whoever built the damn thing just didn't want to have to put too much work into cutting things down to size. It didn't make any sense, but nothing much did, and as long as I didn't think about that, I was going to be just fine and dandy.

My palms went sweaty with that realization—I wiped them off on the skirt of my borrowed dress. The fabric looked dingy, but at least my hands were dry when I went to open the gate; it was more like a door, really, but with four glass panes in it, like you'd be able to look right out and see who'd come for dinner. If that someone wasn't there to strip your meat from your bones. It was a sour little voice in the back of my head that shouted it, and I shoved it aside as I hauled the coop door open. I had work to do, and that was something, at least.

CHAPTER TWELVE

Keep Your Knees Together And Your Doors Locked

ost chickens weren't all that smart. They'd peck the hell out of your ankles if you riled them up—or if you didn't, for that matter, and they plain didn't like you. But my own sad little bunch of birds had known me better than that. I clucked like a biddy hen and stepped into a disconnected moment; I felt like I was in two places at once: fresh from Marty's house, seeing a little pile of blood-speckled feathers, but also inhaling the ammonia of a coop gone too long without a caretaker, black soil instead of dirt, a shelter painted fancy purple like someone had cared more for the outside than for the birds themselves.

There were more than the dozen Granny had mentioned. Ghost birds, chickens I'd watched stop laying until they were scrawny and Marty had fixed them for our dinner, useful to their end. Phantom chickens scratching at bugs. Fat chickens, juice and meat and pride under feathers that were so sleek, I wanted to smooth my hand over them like they were fine dogs or lazy cats resting in a warm patch of sunlight.

My heart gave a double beat, and a pain seized my chest. I had to gasp for my next breath and when I opened my eyes, the chickens I didn't really see—the chickens I Saw instead—weren't there anymore. Just a bunch of black-and-whites who kept to their business when I clucked and minced closer for a better look. Wyandottes. I knew my chickens. Marty had a book about them. They were real pretty, friendly birds, and they laid brown eggs. If they pecked Dell that much, she was doing something wrong. I spotted a couple of plain reliable Sussex hens, too—those were tasty fryers, but it was always a shame to spend one on a meal when they laid so good. Big eggs, real regular.

As many chickens as Granny had, even if they didn't all lay, she'd have plenty of eggs for breakfast and for baking. She'd insisted that I didn't have to go hungry, hadn't she?

The Sussex birds clucked back at me, low and pretty like purring cats. Gossipy old things, telling me the news. My nose twitched again at the smell. My good thoughts about Dell were tempered a bit—if she was the kind willing to let birds sit in their own rank and filth, she might not be as wonderful as I'd kind of decided she was.

I stepped closer to a big fat bird, reached out for it, making soft mama chicken noises even though she'd probably not seen her mama since hatching. Her head tucked under my arm easy as anything and when I rocked her a little, left and right and back and forth, she just kind of eased.

Chickens were the easiest thing in the world to hypnotize.

Maybe that was why we wound up feeding them to the Reborn when we had to. An easy meal. My back felt clammy at the thought, and it made me shiver. I poked at the hen until she woke back up and walked, all high jerky gait and ruffled feathers, over to the water trough.

There was a shallow pool of water at the bottom of it. For the best. Chickens weren't all that smart in general, but they were dumb as anything when it came to water. More than an inch, and they'd drown themselves, I'd seen it. Damn fool birds.

A lean-to in the corner looked to be my best bet for tools. I couldn't clean anything without gloves at the very least. If wishes came true, there'd be a towel to tie over my nose, too. Breathing in chicken dust didn't do anyone any good. Still, if wishes were horses, then Reborn would ride. That hadn't been one of Marty's sayings. I might have got it from my father, even though I couldn't remember him. Made me extra fond of it, for all the Reborn would probably just eat the horse.

There was a latch on the rickety door to the lean-to that, on closer inspection, was really more of a shed slowly falling down to the right and paused to rest against a fencepost before it found the energy to finish collapsing. It looked like it mostly just kept the chickens from poking their beaks in if they got curious; the door wasn't locked. I nosed my way in and found everything I'd need, right down to that wished-for towel. Whoever'd equipped the place knew what they were doing, at least as far as supplies went. Made me think it wasn't Dell.

The birds themselves looked pretty healthy; they were fluffed up and perky, and their legs were clean, at least at first glance. I'd have to go over them to check if there were any mites brewing, but that wasn't any way to say hello. They were going to be upset enough that I had to clean out their boxes, even if they'd appreciate it after the fact. I should have, it occurred to me, asked after who gathered their eggs.

Before getting started, I stood wide and reached between my knees for the back hem of the dress I apparently didn't have much choice about wearing. I bunched it up, then did the same to the front of the hem and tied the fabric together in a loose knot. It made the skirt ride up my thick thighs, but I felt a lot less open to the breeze. That, and it should theoretically prevent the chaffing. Plus, no chicken was going to get tangled up in my skirt and leave me with scratches on any of my sensitive parts. Yep, positives all around. Now, I could just use more of those.

I worked until I was sweaty, slick under my arms and at the crease of my legs and butt. The chickens had all flapped and squawked and wound up as far away from me as they could get, watching and clucking at each other like they just couldn't believe my audacity.

The smell was bad but, as I swept and shoveled, the mess didn't look as old as I'd first thought. Maybe Dell had just been busy, had let it go a little too long between cleanings or something. If she was outside their fence on a regular basis, well, a thing like that could cut into your coop cleaning time. And yes, I was making excuses for her.

But also, something tickled at the back of my throat, it seemed just possible that this had been set up to give me something to do. That made even less sense than anything else, so I swallowed it back and down, sucked the spit off the inside of my cheeks and swallowed again just to make sure that thought stayed in my stomach. If they'd set this up, they'd've needed to get chickens from somewhere. The coop was kind of weird the way it was built up so high, so far over my head, but that little tool shed had to have been leaning there for longer than I had been alive. And they would have needed to know I was coming—there was no way for them to, right? Not unless they knew Marty, or James. If they'd known ahead of time what was going to happen... It wasn't any of it a real worry. It was some kind of paranoia I'd picked up in the woods like a tick.

The idea was in me, though, and it took root in my belly like a watermelon seed. I was going to swell up with it until the leaves came out of my mouth so I might as well just plain ask—Granny or Dell or that boy Jimmy. Young man. Whatever he was. One of them would tell me why the coop was so tall, and then I'd be able to dismiss the rest of the tendrils curling in my throat.

Or not—I fell down to my knees and retched, bile and water and bits of stew I still hadn't finished digesting. Bright green flecks of chewed up pea.

It was the pea that made me laugh. Even in the face of all my troubles, even with a string of spittle dripping off my lower lip before I backhanded it away, I had to laugh at that damn pea. They'd saved my life, but I was bleeding out of one hole and puking out another. I'd probably be sick on the toilet when I got back, just to make it a triple. The smell must have gotten to me more than I realized.

One of the hens clucked her way over and I waved my arm at her—the last thing I needed on top of everything else was chickens with vomit all over them. At least I hadn't put any of the tools away yet. I used the shovel handle to brace myself, hauled my body back upright and wiped my mouth again. My tongue felt dirty, and I wanted a glass of water just as bad as I'd wanted food earlier. It'd have to wait, though. I took some deep breaths through my mouth—the smell of sick mixed with the ammonia might have put me back on my dirty knees again.

Slowly, carefully, I buried my mess, stomped over the cover of dirt to make sure it was all packed down. Then I trudged back to the lean-to that had seemed so charming earlier to put everything back in its spot. Except for the towel. I wiped at my face with it and tucked it under one arm to take it back to the house for cleaning.

Putting things to rights hadn't taken me more than an hour, but it was going on dusk when I put my feet, reluctantly, back across Granny's doorstep. I'd never been very good at estimating time, but I figured it was late enough for supper now. There was no telling how hard that'd treat my stomach, not after the way I hadn't kept anything else down. All the same, I'd gone hungry just long enough that thinking about skipping a meal made me feel kind of panicky.

"Girl, what'd you do to your skirt?" The male voice laughed at me, and I flinched away from it. Jimmy, not Ben, not Ben at all because he was gone and there was no telling if I'd ever see him again, no matter how much I wanted, *needed* that to happen. Jimmy eyed the way I'd knotted the skirt between my legs, the way the fabric had ridden up without me paying it or the rest of me much attention.

I tugged it all back down as much as I could, under his eyes. "It was getting in the way. And I didn't want an angry chicken to get tangled up or something." It had made sense in the chicken yard. In the kitchen, it felt a lot more ridiculous. And no, I wasn't going to explain about the chaffing. My legs were dusty, covered with a fine grit of sand where I brushed my hands over them nervously. I could undo the knot, but I didn't favor squatting open like that to untie it with Jimmy looking at me. The worst part was that it wasn't unpleasant, not when I thought about it. But I wasn't any sort of performer. What I did with my skirt was my business, not so much his.

Ben had looked at Laura like that, like he wanted to pay special attention to her dresses. I shrugged and looked around the kitchen. Pots sat on the stove, at least one of them probably full of those peas Granny had been shucking earlier. I edged around, keeping my face to Jimmy, until the table was between us and I was closer to a door that led deeper into the house. He couldn't see as much anymore. "You know where Granny is? I finished up the chicken coop for the evening, and I want to see if there's anything else I can do for her."

Jimmy blinked all lazy and slow at me. Then he grinned and looked at the table like he wanted me to know he'd seen what I did there. "Yeah, she spilled tomato juice all over herself. She's out changing." He gestured at the collection of pots. "I'm minding dinner for her. You know anything about cooking?"

I felt a little like I'd reacted to something that wasn't even there while he wandered to the stove, in the same low-slung jeans, paired with bare feet and a t-shirt he seemed to have found at the bottom of a pile of something if the wrinkles were anything to go by. Those kinds of looks had been traded all around the school and the general store and anywhere else the town girls had been. I'd even given out a few myself. But no one had returned that sort of thing, not so blatantly with me. It made me want to go back and find Jenny somehow, apologize for how many times I'd thought about kissing her while watching her walk anywhere instead of listening to her talk. Then I'd thank her for letting me kiss her anyway.

The clatter of a metal lid shook me out of my little cloud of guilt; Jimmy had dropped it on the counter and was stirring something that made my mouth water even while it made my stomach clench up. I was having that reaction to a lot of things. And he'd asked me a question.

"I know enough, how not to mess anything up. You need help?" If they were going to give me a place to stay, there had to be more than minding chickens I could do to earn my keep. "What all's she making?"

He glanced back at me over his shoulder, another smile like he was giving them out for free. "Nah, I got a handle on it. Just more stew and some rice and those peas. I don't know what she's going to do with the stewed tomatoes." He wrinkled his nose. "I'd just as soon she threw those out for the hogs."

It startled a laugh from me. "I can't abide the texture." Stewed tomatoes were like... I didn't have anything suitably vile to compare them to. Marty loved the things, poured them over rice at least three times a week.

It seemed like such a mundane thing to find common ground with this strange boy on, but he faked a theatrical shudder, made another face at the thought of them. "I might not have been all that upset when she dropped that pot. Glad she didn't burn herself, but I'm not grieving for the food." He pointed the wooden spoon at me, and something thick and juicy plopped off the end and onto the floor. "That's our little secret though, that okay?"

Jimmy bent down at the knees to wipe up, and I relaxed enough to give him a real smile, a big one. One like I'd have given Jenny if she'd cracked a joke at our teacher's expense. "Cross my heart and so on. She won't be hearing about it from me." I came out from behind the table. "Is there a place for dirty rags? I used this in the coop." I showed him a bit of the towel tucked under my arm. If he'd let me go drop it off, I'd have a chance to untie my dress without him watching me like I was on some carny stage.

I just about sighed with relief when he pointed that spoon again, this time back at the door to the outside. "Utility house is around the side. Just grab another one from the clean pile in there so you've got one for tomorrow if you think you need it."

Wordless, I made my way back out. The utility house, as he'd called it, was really just a tiny little room warm from the lingering sun on its tin roof. There was a washing machine, but there was a big tub and washboard sitting on top of it, too. They might not have the electricity for it out here. It was kind of decadent to run a machine like that off a generator anyway. My foot connected with something, and I looked down at the loud rattle—I'd managed to kick over a bucket of clothespins, and they'd scattered everywhere. I rolled my eyes at myself, jumpy, and set to picking them up.

One had rolled under the washing machine, and I got down on my belly to reach for it. I stretched my arm out, but it was like my muscles protested. I didn't have feelings about things, not as a rule, but there was *something* under that machine, something hunched back against the wall waiting to grab me.

That was the funny part—a rat would bite me for certain, but it wouldn't grab me, and I was afraid of being grabbed. My elbow and my shoulder were ice box cold, but I chipped away at the sensation until my fingers curled around the wooden grain of that clothespin. When I pulled myself back up off the floor, I was fine. Nothing had come after me. I was just being a goose.

I stood up, dusted off my hands on my skirt, and tossed the dirty towel onto a pile of soiled stuff in a hamper by the washing machine. The material was all dark, and the towel was light, but maybe some people didn't sort their laundry the way we had. Or maybe they just didn't have a load of lights ready. It was the little things that kept tripping me up and preventing me from getting too comfortable. I was glad of them, glad to have something reminding me.

When I went to untie my dress, the fabric resisted my fingers—the hem was bunching up and clogging the knot. I picked at it, but threads started to ravel. Machine stitching, it looked like, the fancy serged kind that was supposed to be so stable, but really just seemed like an excuse to look down on those who had to make do by hand or at home on a regular machine. A weird growling distracted me enough to make me raise my head, but the sound lulled and I bent back to it. I didn't want to take too long before getting back to the house—or Jimmy's eyes skipping over the important parts of me like my face if my skirt stayed all up.

The growling started back up, and I flinched, ready to face some kind of unhappy dog. But the door was still closed behind me and the floor was clean. There wasn't a whole lot of clutter, no place for an animal the size of that sound to hide.

My throat was scratchy, had been on and off since the woods. I coughed to clear it, and the roughness of that caught my ears off guard, too. I'd protected my face, but I'd breathed in too much dust back in the coop anyway. I'd get a glass of water in the kitchen once I got this damn knot loose. It finally started to give as I worked it, and I realized that the growling was coming from my own mouth.

CHAPTER THIRTEEN

Don't Count The Eggs In Your Basket

I dropped the fabric and slapped my hands over my mouth. The smell of my fingers almost made me puke again, but I swallowed it back along with the noises. My heartbeat was loud, all I could hear now, and I panted through my nose until my nostrils flared.

One, two, three, I counted in my head. Four, five, six. I kept it up to ten and then counted some more because I'd been breathing too fast, and hyperventilating wasn't going to help me, was just going to get me kicked back out into the woods. I'd been stupid out there in so many ways, but these people weren't my family. I needed to stop trusting them. Especially given what my family had done.

There was too much going on. I needed to stop and think. My hands shook, but I didn't care—I lowered them from my face anyway, smoothed out the crumpled fabric of my skirt. It fell longer, covered my knees instead of just my thighs, and I felt better somehow, safer. Not that Jimmy's eyes had done anything to me; they were just eyes. And he was nice enough. No reason to think he was anything but what he looked like, but no reason to come round to him either, not when I had bigger things to worry about. I was bound and determined to take some kind of action about my situation, not just admire him and how comfortable he made everything look. How easy.

Counting helped, so I did it some more, got all the way up to a hundred and seven before I felt just about as normal as I was going to feel, all things considered. Nothing had grabbed me or bitten me. I was ahead on good things happening to me instead of bad. That was a comforting thought, even taking the growling I'd been doing into account. If I kept any kind of scorecard, that'd be enough to encourage me.

There was a pile of folded towels on another hamper; I grabbed the top one for tomorrow. But I couldn't bite back the scream that tore loose when I picked it up and saw what was underneath. Metal was warm against my back before I even registered that I'd moved—I'd backed away straight into the wall. The door banged open, and Jimmy, wild-eyed and with his hair going every which direction, bolted in. He gave a startled yell when he saw the lanky rat, then grabbed the first thing that came to his hand—a bottle of something, looked like starch, to throw at the pest.

It leapt out of the way, not even scared of the projectile that whizzed over its head, then paused to hiss at us, big teeth bared, before scampering away under the washing machine.

"Holy shit." Jimmy was gasping, like getting around the corner to the utility house had taken something out of him. But, then, as fast as he'd appeared, he had to have sprinted out the second he heard me scream. "Did that thing bite you?"

My breath was doing funny things, too. As much as I'd worked on not hyperventilating before, it appeared I might not have much choice about it at the moment. My inhales were shallow and my exhales panted out hard enough to make me realize how painful and dry my lips were. Things started to blur around the edges and I saw, I Saw Jimmy, stepping toward me with an outstretched hand and a slow, slurred voice telling me to just calm down, everything would be okay if I just calmed down. I blinked back the blurry edges, the red dripping from his fingers, concentrated on his voice. It was warm without making me sweat and all sweet around the edges like he'd taste real good. I kept breathing and registered something in my hands—I was gripping his arm like I'd drown without it. He kept up a steady stream of something low and soothing, more of that morning molasses hum in my ear. The details didn't matter, he could have been telling me about his favorite horse race or last summer's corn crop.

Maybe they grew corn inside the fence. I didn't have any inkling how big the enclosure was, how much ground it really covered. It had to be large to support all the people I'd seen.

Between one breath and the next, I realized that what I needed to do was figure out the boundaries of the thing. Granny had set it down that I couldn't go out; fair. She hadn't given me any rules that meant not being able to follow the fence around on the inside. I gulped lungful after lungful of air until the bands around my chest broke loose. Jimmy's hand rubbed soothing circles on my back, and the heat of his big body crowded up next to me. There wasn't anything hungry on his face, nothing like he was looking down my dress or trying to get a feel of where my breast pressed against his side. He just looked worried, and it made me doubt what I thought I'd seen in the kitchen.

"I'm okay now. I'm okay." My voice still had that rasp in it. "I just... can we get to the kitchen? I need a drink of water."

Jimmy nodded so hard, his head was fair to flopping off his shoulders. But he was steady as he helped me back to my feet. I didn't remember when I dropped into a defensive crouch, but my knees protested being on the ground like that after all the work I'd already done so I must have gone down hard. When I was on my own two feet and not in any danger of falling, I gave him a nod and he took it, kept his hands ready in case I wobbled, backed off to give me some air when I didn't.

"Girl, you can have all the water you want as long as you don't cry or faint. I'm not good with crying or fainting. I'm okay with throwing up, but I've got a whole case of no idea what to do with the others." His laugh was nervous, like a bird in a bush with people walking by. It took flight when I gave him a weak smile, flew up higher under the sun, and I chuckled with him a little. He was okay. I had to give him credit for that. Looking was no crime, and maybe it wasn't so bad to have someone like Jimmy doing the looking anyway. Maybe, I thought, with the clear memory of Seeing his sugar-crusted edges like that, I'd even look back at him.

He made sure the utility house was closed behind us and hovered as I led us back to the kitchen. I clutched that clean towel like it would save my life, but I wasn't sure I could bring myself to use it. It wasn't really clean; it'd been sitting on top of that rat like the roof of a cozy little laundry house. How long had it been there? How long had any of it been there?

As much as I appreciated myself coming up with a plan for my free time, I was not impressed with wondering any of that or thinking about Jimmy. It was all ridiculous notions, just like looking at Dell and pondering how long the coop had been there. People hadn't made these things just for show, just for me. The shed and the utility house—and the main house from what I'd been able to see—were visibly worn down with age. I'd have been set to repair them or knock them down so we could start fresh if they'd been on Marty's property. Apparently Granny had a different take on how long outbuildings could go without some sort of maintenance or repair was all.

It was like Ben was there with me, telling me that maintenance was what kept a farm in order. The difference between us and the town people was that we worked for our living, and part of that was taking care of the things around us, making them last longer. I didn't know anybody else, though. Certainly not Dell or Granny. Maybe even Jimmy had a different attitude about that kind of business.

It occurred to me that a body would be foolish not to remember that when getting involved with either of them. Dell's chickens didn't like her. That told me a lot about a person, more than a pretty turn of the head or a nice tilt to the nose.

I stayed silent while Jimmy fixed me a big glass of water but nodded my appreciation, and he went back to stirring at the pots like we hadn't just gone through all of that. I licked my lips after my first sip, spreading some of the moisture around. I'd gotten too dried out and that could make a body react; I'd have to avoid that in the future.

Dell barreled into the kitchen with another person I didn't know, his arm around her waist. The water went down the wrong pipe when I tried to swallow a gulp of it, and I sputtered and coughed until Jimmy set his spoon back down and Dell was right beside me, pounding on my back. "Just breathed wrong, sorry, sorry." The words came out of me staccato with each stroke of her hand; she was strong, another good thing to remember about her. Probably stronger than me. I told that voice to shut up.

The man Dell had come in with hung back until I stopped coughing and Jimmy took up with the food again like he was washing his hands of us. He was paying that pot more mind than was probably necessary and biting his lip.

"So, you're Dell's stray. I'm Martin." There was something too clean and polished about Martin, something that reminded me of James and his pocket handkerchief. I shook the hand he extended, but I didn't like it. His grip was too firm and his palm cool and soft, smooth with no calluses. He'd had that same hand on Dell's waist, and me? I wouldn't have been able to stand the fish belly feel of it.

I managed a smile out of politeness, even though it was a weak one. "I wouldn't say I'm a stray. I've got all my shots anyway." Marty had carted us into town every year for whatever vaccines the doctor in the government truck had to offer. We'd stood in line with everyone else, our arms bared to get our jabs. I had always felt sore from the needles for a few days afterward, and Ben had gone to bed with a bad sickness for nearly a week one time. But we didn't get the things we were supposed to get, at least we didn't reckon we did.

Jimmy was listening to us—he snickered. Dell outright laughed, but Martin just looked sour, like he could taste the bile that I hadn't managed to quite wash out of my mouth. I took another swig of the water in my glass and grinned.

"That's something, in a place like this. Though I still wouldn't suggest biting the hand that feeds you." Martin's sneer was ugly but fleeting. I inhaled, sharp and surprised, but his expression had already shifted back to something neutral and bland—a mask of smug superiority.

My mouth opened anyway while the rest of me wasn't sure quite how to respond, when Granny bustled in. "Y'all children cut out that racket." Dell and Martin, real obedient, headed through an interior door before I could say anything else. "Make sure you wash your hands before you come back in here." Granny called after them, but I didn't hear anything if they replied. I tucked my own hands under my thighs though. I actually wanted to wash them and didn't need her berating me for uncleanliness.

She eyed me, and I figured she saw what I did. Marty could look through me that same way. But Granny didn't say anything, just edged Jimmy out of the way with her hips. He slung himself into the seat next to me and cut his eyes to the door that started the strange little path to my room.

I squinted back at him, not certain what he was getting at. But Jimmy just rolled his eyes and this time he pointed to me and then to himself and slanted his gaze back to the door. I looked over at Granny's back—she was already humming and stirring things, adjusting the burners so that everything would be ready at once. I blinked, and it clicked what he wanted. "I should wash up before dinner, too. Jimmy, can you show me how the trapdoor latches, please?" His smile was quick and appreciative.

"Yeah, no problem." He stretched when he stood up and waited for me to lead the way. I glanced at Granny again, but she wasn't paying us any mind.

The door creaked shut behind us and Jimmy put a finger to his lips before I could ask what the hell he was playing at. He rambled down the stairs, all rangy limbs, and I couldn't think of anything else to do but follow him.

He stopped at the trapdoor to my room—what was apparently going to be my room. "You need to be careful around Martin."

I frowned at how serious he sounded, no hint of softness around his mouth to indicate he was being unfair. "What do you mean?"

Jimmy crossed his arms, looked uncomfortably contained with his fingers cupping the points of his elbows. "He's a real professional. Likes to make things difficult." He licked his lips, then gnawed on the lower one. "I ain't got much to tell you about it. Just that you don't want to make him mad when you just got here." Jimmy ducked his head at me and turned around to leave before I could even react.

It wouldn't have taken much to stop him. But his warning held my hands still, kept my voice mute. I needed to think on what he'd shared and peppering Jimmy for information he didn't want to give—or maybe couldn't give—wasn't going to help. I shouldered the trapdoor open and headed in to clean up. I fixed to wash at the sink; tidying the coop had been dirty work even before I sweated through my skin in the utility house.

Before I made it to the bathroom, a neat little pile of clothes left on the bed where I'd be sure to find it snagged my attention. That rat was too fresh in my mind for my hands to be anything but wary. But the pile was pretty sizable and, when I actually focused on it, there was a bunch of underthings right on top.

That broke my caution; I rifled through the whole stack of fabric. Two bras roughly close to my size, five pairs of drawers that looked new and felt like they'd been through a wash, and a handful of dresses just about identical to my current hand-me-down. Someone's closet was missing some stuff. But Dell wasn't nearly as thick as I was and Granny was even more birdlike. And it wasn't like they were Jimmy's. If he favored them on his own, they weren't the right size. So, someone else had volunteered up their wardrobe.

Not, that voice informed me, if that person weren't around anymore. They could be dead. Or imaginary—not that imaginary people had closets full of old-fashioned outfits. Plus, if I were the one making the person up, then they'd be wearing pants, damn it.

Between the rat and Martin—who might be a rat all on his own if I believed Jimmy—all the surprise had been shocked out of me for the moment. I sighed, grabbed a clean pair of underpants, a bra, and a dress on the way to the bathroom, then stripped off everything but the drawers and the ring I still wore and started up the tap running with warm water. It heated up fast, and I wet a washcloth, then wrung it out so it wasn't dripping. Under my arms first, where I'd sweated with honest work and then with fear in the laundry room. Over my dusty neck and chest and arms. I rinsed the cloth out; the water ran down dingy into the sink.

Sometimes, at home, it had gotten so dry that bathing was the only hope we had of being comfortable. But it was so wasteful to take baths when the weather was bad. Marty had taught us sink washing; I didn't know if they did the same in town or just used up all the water they felt like using and believed it would never run out. Ben and I had found a little pond that we swam in, but it got warm when the summer was at its worst. The water turned thick and brackish and chock full of tadpoles; I felt slimy every time I dipped a toe in it, but Ben dove in like it was pure refreshment. I stood ankle deep on those days, jumping every time something brushed my ankles.

It was silly, and I'd never told him, but I was also a little bit afraid a tadpole might swim up somewhere it wasn't supposed to. Marty's biology books discredited that kind of thing, insisted frog pregnancies were just superstitious nonsense, but I figured better safe than sorry.

No frogs in this bathroom. I kept wiping until my skin felt eased. The work had helped with my cramps, but I needed a clean pad anyway. Dropping my drawers, I rinsed out the used cloth in the sink. My blood was a little too personal to expect anyone else to scrub off and giving them that kind of material to work with felt dangerous all on its own. Superstitious again, but I used the soap on the side of the sink and washed and rinsed and washed and rinsed until the water ran clear. I laid the pad out to dry on the counter and picked up the washcloth again.

I was sensitive down there, the texture of the cloth rough as I dabbed carefully, head forward and braced one-handed on the counter; it felt good, getting clean, but also just the touch. I'd been running around and scared out of my mind, and then I'd been angry and still scared—I hadn't had room for feeling anything else. No use in dwelling on any of it when I couldn't have done anything about it anyway. We'd never been a real touchy-feely family, but when I looked back, Jimmy putting his hand on my back was the only real contact I'd had since Marty had washed my feet back at the house. My skin got all itchy and goosebumpy when I thought on that. I rinsed the cloth out again, red on white porcelain, then carried it back between my legs.

My ears pricked at every little sound. My luck, Jimmy would walk in on me and then I'd have to die of embarrassment. I didn't doubt he did the same, as much as handling himself was the same, but still. A body liked privacy.

The only things intruding were the muffled sounds from outside and my own breathing, sharp and fast, almost painful. My first thought, when I finished, was that I'd be sore there for at least a day. But the rest of me felt better, looser in my joints, like I'd stretched myself just enough, muscles all clenched and then relaxed.

I rinsed out the cloth again, then soaped it up and gave it a wash-down. My skin cooled, softer all over. I laid the cloth to dry beside the pad, then stripped off my damp underwear. The clean ones I'd brought in with me went on next, a pad fitted into them, then the bra and dress, not much thinking going into it, just letting myself drift a minute. My mouth turned up at the corners without my input as my dirty things got folded up and put in the hamper I'd finally noticed.

The only thing I didn't have a spare of was a pair of shoes. I left my feet bare, figured I'd ask for some shoe polish in the morning to spruce up my own, then made my way back to the kitchen, ready for something like dinner.

CHAPTER FOURTEEN
When In Doubt, Do Nothing

inner was probably, objectively, every bit as tasty as my nose had originally predicted. But my stomach was soured by how awkward and strained it felt to sit at the table, fork in hand. Everything was starting to feel strange to me; too neat and tidy a bookend, to go from Marty's table to this one with the woods in between. I was still all off-kilter.

Dell and Jimmy and Granny and Martin bantered easily enough, like it was a familiar scene. And the fare, cooked like Marty would have made it all slow on the stove with rice cooked in stock and shredded chicken meat, was rich and delicious, oozing a clear, golden puddle of fat around the pile on my plate. Those peas Granny shelled had been cooked with a ham hock, but everything sat like mud in my belly, with an aftertaste of ash. I hadn't seen any pigs inside the fence.

Trees didn't talk; I hadn't spent all that long alone in the grand scheme of things, not when I really stopped to think about it. But getting used to the crowd around the table was an adjustment I hadn't expected to have to make anytime soon. I was listening to all the wrong instincts probably, just waiting for the next thing to go wrong, so I kept my mouth shut, chewed my food, and glanced up enough that no one could say I was being surly.

I must have given off effective enough signals. No one pushed me to be more social, more talky. Jimmy kept looking over at me, and I wondered what he saw or thought he saw. Instead of asking, when we were all done with dinner, I whispered to Granny that I was tired out and headed up to my room, careful not to make eye contact with anyone when I nodded a general goodbye.

Sleep was my friend that night. It came easy and stuck around, and I enjoyed the mattress in spite of my nap earlier in the day.

And the next day happened, started looking like a routine that jarred only because my nerves were strung tight like catgut on a wire fence. The next day happened after that, only the details of our meals different. The sameness kept moving me, a momentum that wasn't mine nudging me along until very nearly adjusted to the new pattern. It was safe and comfortable, but every moment reminded me what I was missing, what I'd come from to get to where I sat. There was a bitter root flavor where I'd expected to find sweet.

Mornings came early, whenever Dell knocked on my door, three sharp raps that roused me and made my feet swing out of the warm covers before my brain even caught up. I spent time with the chickens and gathered their eggs. With a clean coop and regular company, they got generous with their laying, proud about it with a flurry of clucking whenever I came in to greet them. I picked up their eggs carefully, admired each one; I cradled the warm shells in the cup of my palms. The eggs were always pale and creamy though I'd expected them to be brown. Sometimes there'd be a speckled specimen, and I'd hold it to my ear, as it if would let me hear the sea like a shell. I made a sling out of an old towel and carried it with me each morning to transport my findings into the kitchen like I was keeping railroad time.

Granny made pound cakes—butter and sugar and eggs in abundance baked into sweet, dense treats. She cooked us all breakfast, eggs scrambled with sausage though I still never saw any pigs, with soft homemade bread on either side of the sandwich. I was always hungry; it felt like I never filled up. I took Granny at her word and ate without holding myself back, let myself take second helpings when my stomach rumbled at me. Granny didn't say a word, just made sure there were enough pots on the stove. I ate until my belly was tight and ready to bust open.

No one asked me to do it, but a few days in, I picked up the wooden spoon Granny had set down to tend to something else and used it to stir one of the bubbling pots that needed tending. Jimmy gave me a smile, small and pleased, when he came in and saw me standing there. It left me chilly on the back of my neck even as my cheeks heated up.

Marty had tried to teach me to cook. That felt farther away than I could imagine. All my failures at it didn't matter anymore because I wasn't sure that kitchen had ever even existed. I stirred and simmered.

The next day, people came to the door, nosing for lunch, looking at me like I'd been a break in their habit, and I realized that I must have actually been—no one had stopped by because Granny waited for me to settle like dust. These were people I might have seen on that first, wide-eyed walk to her house, but that memory was just one long hunger pang now. The more food we made, the more people showed up to eat it without there seeming to be any system of communicating about it. There were always enough folks to eat up all the food, and there was always enough food to make sure everyone got everything they wanted. Instead of trying to figure it out, I put faces in my mind, tried for names even as I wondered if knowing them would make any difference.

Everyone seemed to know who I was, and they called me Dell's stray no matter how much I told them to call me Hank or not to call me at all. All those people made for a lot of dishes, so I helped wash and dry and put away, and that counted as my afternoon chores.

Once the dishes were done, I was at loose ends. I took to following the fence, keeping to my half-formed plan I'd made back when Jimmy had his hand on me. The more I walked, the bigger and wider and taller it seemed, and the more like a real town the compound looked. The curve of the fence was just the inside of what I'd stumbled along, trying to keep up with Dell, always curving just slightly toward me this time instead of away. Twice, I met fence inspectors, carrying their guns like they knew how to use them, coming from the opposite direction. I stood back for those men, well back from the fence and watched as they ran eyes and fingers over every inch, checking for some invisible breach. I never did see a gap, never even the hint of a dent. And no matter how far I followed it in an afternoon, the fence stayed the same.

I wasn't good enough to calculate the area it covered; Ben had been better at that sort of math than me. I did accounting, added up the money even though he handed it over at the store.

But that area wasn't empty space; I wasn't tromping through more scrub and wilderness. There were houses, more of them like Granny's place and the ones there, with open doors and no windows. Maybe, secret passageways, too, lonesome rooms at the end of weird tunnels waiting for more people to be rescued from outside the fence. Was my room actually in one of those houses? There just wasn't any way for it to fit in Granny's even though the tunnel wasn't very long. Nothing about this place was normal, so maybe that wasn't normal either, maybe houses upstairs didn't need to have a thing to do with spaces downstairs.

That blue door, the one I passed behind Granny's house on my way out to the chicken coop every morning—that blue door caught my attention every chance it got, and I started to think of it, for some reason, as my real front door. Just let someone come knocking.

The houses weren't empty, not that I'd expected them to be. The people were friendly without offering friendship, a particular trick I'd never gotten the hang of when it came to the townies at home. These people were more reserved, so keeping the barriers between us came more naturally. I hoped Jelly and the Gentrys and even Seymour and his crew were faring well.

There still seemed to be more houses than people, and once I got better at identifying who was coming to lunch, I started seeing the same faces at different houses. That might have been part of why they were reserved, but I noticed just the same and tucked that away in the spot in my mind that wasn't thinking about anything.

Names came last, the way names always do. Hector had hair thicker than mine, black and straight, and he always looked like he knew a secret. Elizabeth wore her blond hair in a bun, and her skin was sunburnt copper. Her eyes were green and cloudy—a prophet if ever

I'd seen one. Dell caught me standing in a corner, staring. "Cataracts," she whispered. But Elizabeth never needed help to navigate a crowded room. There was also Marta in men's overalls, and I wanted to talk to her about that, even though she seemed happy not to talk to anyone at all.

There were others. I would think about writing their names down, and then the thought would slide right out of my head by the time lunch rolled to a close, my hands sunk down in the sink full of water, too busy for using a pencil in any kind of way.

And there were others beyond that. I'd noticed, when I walked into town, that everyone was different. I didn't know the logic that kept five big men out on the wrong side of Granny's threshold, but I handed them sack lunches instead of watching them slog inside. I kept my own tongue in my mouth and added it to the list of things about Granny and Dell that didn't add up.

They were good to take care of me. I thought about that when I thought about anything. But they weren't necessarily good people. I thought about that when I couldn't help myself. I tried to remember it, but the hum of normalcy drowned out that little bit of mosquito noise. I didn't feel hypnotized—more like I had a head cold and was walking around pretending to be well.

Jimmy was always there, every day, more often than Dell. I caught fleeting glimpses of her, smiles she'd give in greeting or farewell, and kept me looking after her long after she was gone. She didn't come back for lunch. When I asked, Jimmy scoffed and I had to figure out on my own that she spent most of her time outside the fence, looking for trouble on foot. I got used to Jimmy instead, all jeans and boots and no shirt until I wondered if he even owned any. He had constellations of freckles on his shoulders, and they seemed to have spread every morning when I looked at him.

The only time I felt awake was when I was heading out to the gate. The usual friendly distance got sharper and colder there, though I never did run into a crowd. I didn't try to leave—I had Granny's warning to keep me company but, more than that, I had my memory of those bony fingers waiting to catch me. Instead, I just tried to make eye contact. Something that small would have felt like a victory with the guards—I wanted them to know me, the way they knew Dell by sight. Them finding me familiar would be a good start, especially if they'd acknowledge me. They never seemed to focus their gaze on anyone inside though; they scanned, and then turned back to face the outside, always shady and darker because of the trees. I couldn't tell if they saw me at all.

Not that knowing me on any level would stop them from shooting me if I gave them any kind of excuse. They stood like they were ready for a whole herd of Reborn to come at them through the gate. Maybe it had before, I didn't know and no one was talking.

No one was talking, but I wanted that feeling of being awake. And after a steady week and a half of visiting the gate, I saw something I had not expected. Martin didn't see me, entirely focused on the person whose arm he was clutching, not just clutching but dragging in through the gate, grip tight and painful on the boy's bicep. The boy looked to be younger than me, his face pale and his red hair sticking up like he'd met a scuffle. There was a mark on his face like that, too. I didn't recognize him. The guards stepped clear of Martin's path, didn't even offer him a token challenge, and I followed the pair without thinking about it.

I kept my distance. I might not have been thinking entirely, but I wasn't stupid either and I had been out and about for the morning enough not to feel so dreamy. Martin made me nervous, made me feel sharper, reminded me even more of James this time around. He made his way deeper into town, and I kept close to walls and corners until the houses gave out and I wanted to slap myself silly. I'd been so focused on the fence that I hadn't checked the middle of town. And sitting here at the heart of things was a tidy little building that looked as official as they came.

A flag flapped in the breeze. Martin dragged his companion past the pole and headed for the door. I hadn't grown up thinking much about the government, though Marty's story put all that in a different light. There were debates sometimes, the kinds of things that happened on front porches and during town picnics, about what the Feds ought to be doing, mostly about what they ought to be doing about the Reborn. Folks talked about how they ought to be hunted down, how there ought to be a nationwide network of roads instead of just the state ones, how there needed to be better schools. The old, familiar topics, rehashed all my life, people changing sides as their comfort levels waxed and waned. We didn't have a flag in town, weren't big enough for a train schedule anymore.

If Martin paid attention in that minute, he'd have spotted me in a heartbeat. I didn't have any practice in sneaking around, just that one night when Ben and I had headed to Seymour's tent. And it was debatable how well that had turned out. Something still nagged me about it, made me think Seymour's visit had truly been the start of all the trouble even though James had been the one to take Ben away.

The building itself was plain and made of the same wood the houses were—long planks that lapped over each other like waves rolling down the wall. But the exterior was painted, white and clean, the cleanest, brightest thing I had ever seen, it felt like. It looked bigger than a town with only the number of people I'd counted would need, unless they were hiding more people in it. The whole place was starting to feel like that to me, like it would have been foolish of them to build so much for so few, so there had to be more. That voice irked at the back of my brain again; maybe, like so many of the other things I tried to ignore, this building was an illusion.

Martin and the boy disappeared through the front door; I was close enough to hear the heavy slam of it closing behind them. There were no windows, like every other place I'd seen, so I crept closer. They were inside, and that meant they couldn't see me, so there was no reason to keep my distance. It didn't feel right though, and I paused at the flag pole. A brass plaque set into the ground at its base read: Government Station 12. Whatever that meant, it didn't seem good.

There was no sign on the building itself, no indication of what it might be used for other than that plaque, which seemed to me to mean at least eleven other buildings like this one stood scattered around, though I had no idea where they were. I wanted it to be some kind of town hall, that would be easy and reassuring. I set my hand against the door, considered testing, seeing if I could push my way inside. The painted wood chilled my hand, smooth and strange after the familiar roughness. Whatever went on in there, I didn't want to face Martin unexpectedly. If he figured out I'd been following him, I'd end up on his bad side for sure—I remembered Jimmy's warning, kept it in the forefront of my mind. I slid my hand down that cool paint and then jumped when something sharp caught me. A nail, sticking through from the backside of the door, holding something fast to it that I didn't want to imagine. My feet backed me away, shame clogged my throat, and I scurried back to the outskirts, where things were comfortable, where my days were easy and foggy.

Where, I dug my nails into my palms against admitting, it felt like I belonged.

Granny's house was quiet when I made it back, everyone busy with afternoon things. I slipped in through the open door to the kitchen. The door never seemed to be locked, and if there was another door from the outside in, I hadn't seen it. I headed for the pantry, looking for something to settle me in place, keep my stomach where it needed to be. An apple and some day-old bread, tough on the outside but still soft and chewy on the inside, were good enough for me. I sat down at the table, unwilling to be alone in my room, and scuffed the sole of one bare foot against the opposite leg. My head felt clear for once, my mind doing what I wanted as I turned things over. That boy hadn't been willing to be there. And I hadn't helped him. Hadn't known how to help. Hadn't known how to help Ben when James dragged him into a similar building, hand gripped tight around Ben's arm, the same arm Ben would sling around my shoulders in casual affection.

Even so, the rest of the day passed before I realized it. Every time I blinked, more time ticked by than should have been possible. Not unlike the dust storm, the way the whole night had passed in between breaths. I looked up, my heart in my ears, and Granny was through the door, a bag over her shoulder bulging with whatever she brought home from wherever she had been. She didn't give any sign that I surprised her—in fact, she didn't give any sign that she saw I was there. I frowned down at the table and when I looked back up, Jimmy laughed with her at the stove, the corners of a kitchen towel tucked into the front pockets of his jeans like a makeshift apron, his speckled shoulders shifting as he mixed up some batter in a bowl. Dell came in and was gone again, and it was all enough of a dream that I wondered if I'd gone somewhere and fallen asleep.

Instead, finally, I shifted my chair, scraped wood over wood with a squeal of friction. Granny and Jimmy both jumped, and Granny put a hand to her throat. "Lands, girl." She settled quick, but Jimmy had to put his hands on his knees and laugh until he could breathe again.

Granny slapped him between his sharp shoulder blades, and he straightened back up with one last chuckle. "Where'd you come from?" He cocked an eyebrow, and my cheeks heated up.

"Y'all were busy at the stove." It was only a half truth and something in me cringed to give it to Jimmy. But Granny was right there and the flapping of that flag had unnerved me something awful anyway. Martin's grip on that boy's arm, the boy's scuffed up face—none of it spoke well of what I'd glimpsed. If I could get Jimmy alone later, maybe take a walk around the outside after dinner, I'd confess what I'd seen and what I hadn't done.

As much as Dell caught my eye and held my gaze, I trusted Jimmy more. That stung. I opened and closed my mouth at the realization, and his head tilted at me. He flicked a look at Granny's back, where she industriously stirred a stock in progress, then nodded, deliberate and understanding.

I got up from the table, fussed around like I was tidying. "Didn't mean to give you a fright, Granny."

She laughed at me, and there was no clear sign if she believed me. Just had to go on acting like she did though, and see what happened next. "You might have done better on your own than I gave you credit for, creeping around like that." Granny gave me a look from the corners of her eyes. "Course, then we'd have to do without you here, and that'd be a shame, wouldn't it?"

I wasn't doing all that much, at least it didn't seem that way to me. But I wasn't about to argue. "I know I'd be regretful." Seemed like a bad idea to sound ungrateful, and Marty had been firm on how it was never a bad idea to say thank you. "I still appreciate you making a place for me."

We all moved around the kitchen in comfortable silence. I kept looking over at Jimmy, but every time we made eye contact, I skittered away from it.

"If y'all are going to keep making eyes at each other, you can just get right on out of my hair." Granny didn't turn from her position at the stove. I startled. I'd been thinking we were more subtle than that, even though she'd got the wrong end of the stick, thinking we were sparking.

The breath hissed out of me—did Jimmy think the same thing? I'd thought his nod meant he understood I had something to tell him. Was he reading more into this than I'd meant to put there? Was there something in his level gaze I didn't recognize? I hadn't had a lot of practice. Jenny had been obvious—I'd looked at her, and she'd cut a sly glance my way, and then she'd kissed me once we'd made our way a little distance from the annual picnic. We'd tasted each other's mouths behind the post office while everyone else celebrated another year in the middle of town.

Jimmy's ears had pinked up and his eyes widened when I made myself look over at him. He set his shoulders, muscles stiff. "That sounds good to me, Granny, if you don't mind. Hank, you fancy taking a walk?"

My mug heated up, and I couldn't look at his again. It wasn't that the tabletop was so interesting—I just couldn't tell if he was being serious or just taking advantage of the opportunity Granny had unwittingly given us. I cleared my throat. "That sounds real nice, actually. I'd be pleased."

We stuttered back and forth on our feet for a minute, both of us trying to figure out who needed to take the first step outside.

Evidently, I had less patience than he did—I rolled my eyes and headed for the door. He fell into step a bit behind me, and we were silent as I led us around back by the chicken coop. The clucking of the birds was soothing. He smiled a little at one particular bird coming up to the fence, bold as anything. It was enough to break the ice between us.

"I think you're pretty and all." He blushed, all the way down across the freckles on his collarbones.

I opened my mouth to try to let him down some degree of easy—I liked him, and I kept looking at him, but I didn't think I liked him like that—but he shook his head and I kept quiet, gave him a chance to figure out what order he wanted to put his words in. Jimmy didn't talk a whole lot, so it was only polite.

"That ain't why I asked if you wanted to go for a walk, though. I know you were in the kitchen, at the table, the whole time. There's no way we'd have managed to miss you coming inside or downstairs." That was a long speech from him.

And I shouldn't have been so surprised—Jimmy kept his eyes on things, too. Maybe, he had the Sight, too, but I definitely wasn't going to ask him about that. It was too personal, not something folks ever talked about though enough people had to have it, for stories to go around like that until everyone knew it existed. Dell didn't seem the kind—she kept her eyes open when she was outside, at least from what I'd seen, but in the house, she always seemed to have a lazy feel about her. Neither she nor Granny paid much attention inside the house—it was a safe place for them. Jimmy's attention was different, felt like he couldn't just turn it off.

And Jimmy was waiting on some response from me—I gave him the nod he expected. At least, he trusted me not to bother lying to him. "I was at the table. Been sitting there for a good long time, but I don't even know how long, because time felt funny, like it wasn't counting me the way I should have been counting it."

That barely made sense to me, but he didn't look confused or surprised or any of the things I felt. His eyebrows eased up like I'd confirmed something for him, a thing he'd been suspecting but wasn't sure he wanted to be true. "Was it like you couldn't move? Like something heavy swimming in your lungs until you thought you were drowning?"

That first part sounded about right, but I'd been breathing fine. Or had I? I couldn't remember if I'd breathed any breath at all, though I had to have or I'd have passed out. "I just sat there. But there wasn't anything in my chest that I know of. More like someone had hold of my head between their hands, with their fingers over my eyes while I remembered stuff."

That got his eyebrows up, but then he nodded again. "It takes everyone different."

It took a minute to understand what he meant. "It happens to you, too?" If it did, maybe it was all real and I could stop lying to myself when I shoved the things I was noticing back under the covers of my mind. Maybe it was all just normal and I was worrying over nothing. Though the way Martin had gripped that boy's arm didn't feel like nothing. It made me uneasy.

Jimmy seemed nervous all of a sudden, looked over his shoulder and, when he spoke next, muttered under his breath so that only I could hear. "Just be careful what you eat around here. No reason to go hungry, but pay some attention is what I mean."

I didn't really have any adequate response to that—and he didn't wait for one. Jimmy leaned close, patted my shoulder like he'd had to think about how to touch another person, then turned and headed back toward the house. He stopped after a few steps, came close to looking back at me, and waited. It'd look funny if we didn't go back into the kitchen together, he was right about that without saying anything to me at all; I had to appreciate the point.

But his other point just didn't make any damn sense. Watch what I ate—we all ate the same thing. And he helped cook it. So did I these days.

I heaved a sigh and caught up with him. Jimmy kept his eyes forward but walked close enough that he kind of bumped up against me a couple times, less deliberate than that pat on the shoulder, and nicer, too. I didn't move away. I was confused enough about him. But, it was weird, that confusion gave me a little space to think about everything else.

Nothing good was going on in Government Station 12, there couldn't be. When I thought about it with a clear head, I could even make some guesses as to what it was being used for. That boy wasn't coming back out the same way he went in. And, if I were going to guess, this wasn't a real natural damn town. Everything looked strange, nothing looked lived in. And, I realized something that had been bothering me from the start, it was too far from the main road to have grown up on its own. It had all been built by someone who was trying too hard. The coop—that thing wasn't intended just for chickens. And there weren't enough people—but if they worked for the government, then there didn't have to be as many people doing jobs as we had in Wanton.

If they worked for the government, maybe everything really had been a sham from day one.

Jimmy gave me a funny look as I stumbled over my own feet. "You okay?"

"It's nothing. Just a root." He'd been kind to warn me about Martin and whatever he was trying to warn me about now. Honest enough to tell me I wasn't the only one slipping time. But that didn't mean Jimmy was what he looked like no matter how many shirts he didn't wear. And Dell, too. She'd brought me here—had she known where to go looking for me in the first place?

Had Marty set me out so they'd find me instead of me finding a train north?

I didn't know the answers, but some of them had to be inside Government Station 12. My days were mostly unminded. All I had to do was keep acting like I'd been acting. And maybe get into that damn building for a look.

CHAPTER FIFTEEN

An Apple A Day

My thoughts ate more of my stomach than I did of my dinner until I felt sour and nervous. I pushed my food around on my plate, wondering at what it might really be until Granny looked at me and frowned when she saw the mess I'd made of my piece of bread, torn into tiny pieces like confetti. Jimmy looked at me, too. He looked more like I'd kicked his puppy though, all sad eyes and downcast glances. Didn't mean he put a shirt on, so he couldn't have felt too badly about everything.

It might have been beef in that stew. Might have been horse. But I was starting to get real suspicious about it and about the easy way everyone else at the table had with it, like they were filling up without paying much attention to their plates, without stopping to think about what was going in their mouths because they'd eaten enough of it to be immune, had exposed themselves to enough of it not to worry. There was no telling for sure what it actually was, and I didn't want to think about it too much.

I went to bed early. I thought I'd go right to sleep, even with my thoughts swirling—I hadn't had any trouble on previous nights. The uncomfortable truth was that I was usually too tired to worry about anything other than getting into bed before I dozed off. But I couldn't get my pillows right; they kept having lumps where they should have had squish. The covers all tangled in my legs. I was too hot. But when I shook off the blankets, I was too cold. And sleeping with just the thin sheet made me feel like I was setting myself up as bait in a trap. It was too dark and still for me to be reasonable about anything. I tossed and turned for a while longer, then climbed out of bed to wet my forehead with a rag.

All it did was just make me clammy once I climbed back under the covers. But I had to have fallen asleep at some point because I jerked back awake, aware mostly of a burning need to pee and little else. It felt later than I'd slept before, and I stumbled to the bathroom. When I caught a glimpse of myself in the mirror, my eyes looked big and bright, but my cheeks were white as anything except for two spots of red riding high on them. I did my business and washed my face. Marty would know what to do, but Marty wasn't here. Granny. Granny, not Marty. Still, she'd know just the same.

My nightgown hung limp down my legs, and I wished for my old pants even as I realized I'd sweated through the fabric during the night. I needed Granny even if I didn't trust her.

Halfway to the kitchen, I had to stop and lean against the wall, panting. I stopped twice more before I made what seemed like a longer trip than it had ever been. I had no idea what time it was but was still surprised to find her sitting at the table. Her eyes opened wide at me. "Girl, what's the matter with you?"

I opened my mouth to tell her I didn't think dinner had agreed with me, but nothing came out other than air. And then the room slid onto its side and I felt the floor under the ragged skin of my cheek. It was better than my bed had been—the floor stayed where it was supposed to once it stood up to say hello. I let my eyes slip closed and went back to sleep.

I didn't dream anything, but when I woke up, something held me down. I flailed and tried to kick out, but it was just covers, a heavy blanket on top of the comforter. I wasn't so desperate once I knew what it was keeping me on my back, and it felt safe and tight. Instead of fighting, I let myself slide back under my eyelids. I wasn't drowning. No one forced me to eat anything. I couldn't tell if that was a memory or a dream, and I was too tired for it to matter much.

The next time I woke up, I looked around with a distant, blunted curiosity. It wasn't my room. The light was dim, just enough to make out the details in all the furniture. No windows, but there never were in this town, fewer even than there had been before, wherever I'd been before, and the lack of that memory didn't stir me up. A small lamp burned low next to me like a nightlight. I was on a heavy, four-poster bed.

Something about it all made me think of the sea even though there wasn't enough light to pick out any color. Still, the walls had to be blue. More wood than just the bed, too—thick beams crossed the ceiling that came down into posts at each of the corners. There might also have been something else I should see and worry about—something kept catching at me like I was walking through bushes with stickers on them—but I couldn't make my head focus on any one thing. I thought my head had been clear before, whatever had come before. In the end, I looked around and I forgot that it had reminded me of something.

Even the door was the same heavy wood, dark and deep-grained. Detached, I wondered what the wood was, then remembered the steps of a house I couldn't recall in more detail: cypress. Wherever that house was, whoever it belonged to, I was never going to see them again. That was a surprising pain, and I worked harder to remember—there were faces, and finally, there were names. Marty. And Ben. And I hadn't been able to even say goodbye.

How I'd forgotten their names I had no idea, but the rush of them coming back hurt in my chest so much, it startled tears out of me that I hadn't even shed in the woods. In this bed I didn't recognize, with the chill of fever still making my bones ache, I gave in and had to turn myself over so I could hide my face against a pillow. Wouldn't do for anyone to hear. I was on my own, so I had to be on my own. That had a familiar ring to it, but I didn't know if it came from before or after, from Marty or Granny. I was on my own, and I was in danger. My memory wasn't working the way I was used to it working, the easy way where it just gave me what I wanted. I struggled to throw the blankets back so I could sit up, but the room spun around me—and the door opened. Dell eased in, a tray in her arms.

Her, I recognized, I noted bitterly. No memory issues there.

"You're awake. That's a good sign—we were worried your fever had gotten too high." Dell thumped the tray down on a sideboard and moved to block me before I could swing my legs out of the bed. "Hey now, you lay back. You're still on bed rest."

Bed rest wasn't me taking care of myself—it was just letting the fog creep back into my head, until I couldn't remember anything about where I came from. And, even in this situation with only half my sense to go on, I knew that'd be bad. I fought her, tried to at any rate, even through my weakness. She pushed me back against the pillows with a firm hand to my chest; I'd known she was stronger than me on a good day. And then the temptation set in because she was tucking the blankets back up around me and I was warm instead of freezing cold.

"You stay there now." She pointed a strict finger at my nose. I went cross-eyed trying to focus on it. She paused, waited to see what I would do, and when I didn't move, she went and retrieved the tray. There was a glass of water on it and a deep bowl of something I could almost smell through the cotton stuffed in my head.

Even without smelling that food all the way, my body let me know in no uncertain terms that it was hungry—my stomach reared up like it was going to go over there and eat without taking me along. Which would have been a thing to see, but I preferred to keep my organs in my belly.

It was a strange thought.

Dell settled the tray on the bed next to me, then hitched her hip up on the side so she could sit. "I'm going to feed you, and you're going to shut up and eat it, right?"

Her tone didn't leave me a whole lot of room for arguing even if I had been stronger. And I didn't want her to take the food away, so I just nodded. She checked to see if I was going to behave myself, then fussed around with tucking a napkin under my chin. Finally, she picked up a spoon, and it was all good to me.

The bowl was full of a stew, something dark and rich and meaty. It steamed lightly, probably fresh from the big pot on the stove that

Granny always had something cooking in. It didn't look like there were any vegetables, not even potatoes; the thick gravy dripped slow off the bottom of the spoon when Dell loaded it up and raised it to my mouth. "Open up, Hank."

There had always been vegetables in Granny's stews, cutting the richness with starch. They'd give under my teeth without resistance, different from the meat but without challenge, without jarring what my mouth expected to feel. This wasn't right, wasn't the way dinner was supposed to be. This was what Jimmy had meant—I remembered Jimmy now—when he told me to mind what I ate.

But I opened up just the same, Dell and my hunger working in concert. The first mouthful blasted my head like wind down the street. I was hit with the smell of it—meat and spice. Iron. Pepper. The liquid burned my lips, but the meat itself was tender, shreds falling apart under Dell's spoon so that I barely had to chew them. Granny knew how to cook no matter what she cooked, no matter what this was, and I still didn't know. Didn't *want* to know. I tried to savor it, but my belly was having none of that; I made a show of chewing and swallowing, except I didn't take my time, and then Dell was there with the next spoonful. I kept it up, like the second hand on a clock, until she scraped the bottom of the bowl with the side of the spoon to get up the last dregs. I closed my mouth around the spoon for a moment, held on and let the metal taste register so that I could tell myself I was done. At least for the moment.

"How's our hospitality taste, Hank?" Dell smiled down at me, but the question seemed off. She plucked the napkin from where she'd tucked it in, then used it to wipe up a smear near the corner of my mouth. She tidied up, spoon in bowl and napkin back on tray, then stood to move the whole thing back to the sideboard by the door. She didn't seem to be expecting an answer at least.

That was good because I wasn't sure I could have summoned one up. I was sinking into my own full belly, my body relaxing, everything I'd remembered a little more faint and not as pressing. There was a little spasm at the small of my back; I shifted as much as I could, which squirmed me deeper into the mattress. My back eased up, and the rest of my muscles followed. My eyes felt heavy, and Dell didn't wait for a response. I could hear her moving around the room, but I couldn't tell what she was doing.

And then I was asleep again. I couldn't tell, when I woke up, if I had slept and woken before or if I had dreamed about it, maybe more than a few times. Or had I dreamed about what was going to happen this time? Dell came over and settled the tray on the bed next to me, hitched her hip up to sit down before she tucked a napkin under my chin. The stew looked the same, a slick of grease across the surface before she broke the tension by giving it a stir. The spoon came back out, dripping slow, and I opened for it, chewed and swallowed. Repeated like it had happened before until the bowl was empty.

This time, though, she didn't get up and maybe it hadn't all been a dream after all because I hadn't dreamed about her taking my right hand and turning it over so that the back of it was cradled in her palm.

"This here's your lifeline." She ran a fingernail, shapely and clean though I didn't know how she managed it with all her wandering around outside, across the line, catching on all my calluses and dry skin. There was a cut I didn't remember getting, right on the meat of my palm, scabbed up in a healing itch. Dell rubbed her thumb over it until I shivered, but she couldn't distract me from remembering where I'd heard those words before.

I wasn't cold. I'd kissed Jenny back in Wanton and felt the same shiver before I'd ever come to Government Station 12. That's maybe where I was now—I remembered the sign. I remembered Marty and the rest of it, and I knew that she had lied to me, but maybe she hadn't thought it was a lie. And I'd touched the door of that building, and it was like I'd been infected with something, though I knew that wasn't possible. Right?

Marty'd had a book about how things got infected. Clean painted wood couldn't make me pass out like that, couldn't give me a fever until I lost my senses. This was something else, something Jimmy had tried to warn me about, something making my head fuzzy and my belly empty. Something in all those dinners I'd eaten with them, the food they were used to that I'd never had before. Dell offered to read me my palm, but now I knew what the difference was. None of them had the Sight. However she went about it, it wasn't real.

"I've had my palm read before." Marty had looked at my other palm, told me my lifeline was long and healthy. Dell just smiled at me. She ran her whole thumb over my palm this time, like it was a caress.

"They tell you then that your lifeline is long and deep?" Her nail rested again the blank spot where my lifeline broke. "You've got a lot of life ahead of you, Hank. And an interesting one, I'd bet." She cocked her head to one side and leaned in closer to get a better look. "It won't be quiet. But I bet you already knew that, too."

I could have told her that without looking at my damn hand. And all I'd need to go on was everything that had happened since James came to dinner. I snorted, light as I could—I was glad to remember his name all of a sudden, and I didn't want to actually be rude to her. But I didn't have any energy for faith in her fortune telling, not when she was touching my hand the way Ben had touched Laura's. I'd have been interested in that if she'd done it back by the water. Now I just wanted her to let me go. I tried to pull my hand back.

Dell's mouth flattened out like I'd insulted her. And maybe I had, maybe she could tell I didn't believe she had any power; her expression smoothed out into a smile that didn't feel real before I could press her on it. That first expression had been the more honest one, but she'd had practice at hiding what she was feeling. Even so, she patted my arm before picking the tray back up and leaving me to sleep more. That flat mouth, that was the most honest she'd been with me and that told me this was all real, none of it dreams. While I'd been making half-hearted eyes at her, she'd been making masks at me, pretending to be friendly when she had something else she was trying to get at.

It took me longer to get back to sleep than it had all those other times before. As pleasant as my full belly was, it was also a little uncomfortable, my digestion gurgling efficiently no matter what I turned over in my mind. It was like I was a little too much for my own skin now, and Jimmy's warning rang in my ears. I hadn't even asked what was on the menu, I'd just opened my fool mouth and ate. I sighed, left my hands tucked up on the curve of my distended stomach. Let my mind wander, dip back into soft, cottony darkness where everything felt safe even though I knew it wasn't. I was going to need my energy for whatever came next.

•

CHAPTER SIXTEEN

Feed A Fever

There was no clock in the room. I looked for one the next time I woke up with no idea of how long I'd slept, no idea how long I'd actually been in this damn room in the first place. It was starting to feel like all of the other time I'd spent with the freedom to come and go from that trapdoor room had been the fever and this was the reality, somewhere I'd woken up after running out of Marty's place. Still, my mind sharpened again, and I felt like if I just had a minute or two to think, I'd be able to put things together.

She'd made me leave, Marty had. I wouldn't have left on my own. I'd spent my nights in the woods though that was a bad idea for a reason that escaped me at the moment. And then I'd found Dell. Or she'd found me. I'd been in a dust storm, and thirsty, and she'd brought me to Granny for a glass of water. I'd lived with them, all my questions unspoken because I was afraid to ask, and I'd taken care of their birds in a coop that looked like someone had built it from a picture in a book without ever having met a chicken in their life. Or, I remembered an old thought, that looked like it was meant to contain something entirely different than chickens in the first place.

And then I'd followed Martin to that building in the center of town and neither he nor that boy had come out after Martin had hauled his captive inside. I had thought that building was the center of the danger. But I was here, and I should be afraid, captive myself.

That was a new idea, and it tolled in me like a church bell. The noise was an anchor and it tethered me where I'd been all set to float away. I shook my head, like that would clear it even more; there wasn't anything but rumors back in Wanton and even those were half-formed at best. Who were these people, and what was that job Granny had mentioned when I arrived? No mail train carried the letters in that unmarked box this deep into the backwoods, but I'd never seen Dell or anyone in town to collect them either.

My stomach throbbed with emptiness in time with every realization. I needed to eat. They'd promised I never had to go hungry. Jimmy had repeated it, like it was extra important, that afternoon when we'd taken a walk. No telling when that was, and it didn't matter so much, as long as I got something in my mouth soon, something between my teeth. No telling anything anymore though, not locked in this room, wrapped up in bed while I waited for someone to come feed me like a baby.

But I wasn't weak with sickness anymore. I wanted to be smart so I tried to plan. If everything went the way it had been going, Dell would come in with food for me. That was good. I was still sick, that much was obvious. I didn't feel normal. I'd ask her about a doctor, if they had any. Feed a fever, starve a Reborn, Marty had recited time and again, so I'd eat until I didn't feel shadows in my vision anymore. The Sight always made people susceptible to turning, always made it easier to see through the veil. Marty'd put me out when I needed her the most, but she'd raised me good, told me things I needed to know. That's how I'd survive.

Dell would open the door, and I would eat. I'd eat until I felt strong again. And then I'd find out what was going on in that damn building. Unless I was there now—that was the other alternative, the option I didn't want to consider. But once I thought that thought, it stuck around and wouldn't shake out. I didn't try this time, didn't stuff it down the way I had so many irksome things. Instead, I let it sit in front of my eyes and turned it around and around. Things were too blue in this room. Not government looking enough.

The door opened—as predicted and as highly anticipated. My stomach grumbled and my mouth started watering, well trained both of them. I'd have been embarrassed if I had any more room for that kind of thing in my head.

Eating felt like a ritual now. Dell sat down, just as she'd done before, as though she'd done it a hundred times and would do it a hundred times more. Maybe she had. Maybe she'd done this for other strays in the woods that she'd brought home and claimed. The gravy dripped off the spoon, slow and thick, almost like molasses. It tasted the same, rich and meaty, sweet like bacon, an undertone of metal in the broth.

The warmth of it spread through me, down my throat and filling up my pelvis. I broke with tradition as a cramp rolled through me. Had I been there a whole month? "Might be that the stew's gone off." I felt just as warm all over as I had before—no chills, no sweats, nothing but that cramp making me feel like someone grabbed my guts and twisted them around. But even as I spoke, I wanted what was left in the bowl, leaned in for it and Dell didn't keep it back from me, didn't answer with anything other than the last spoonful scooped up and fed to me even as I shook and wrapped my arms around my middle.

I didn't ask for that nice little stack of cloth pads. I knew what they'd done when another cramp hit. They'd given me bad meat. And they'd done it on purpose. I saw it so clear, my only regret was not figuring it out sooner when they were fattening me up on the same kind of meat they ate. The same kind of meat Reborn ate.

Prey. Human meat. And then, the process started, from that very first meal Granny had served me.

They couldn't have been eating all that much of the tainted meat. I couldn't imagine how many bodies they'd have had to go through if they were. But it was like the edges of a picture were coming into focus now, and the answer was, they had to just be mixing it in a little bit, just enough to get me used to it. Or to see if it would make me ravenous.

If anyone had asked me, I'd have expected more Seeing to be involved in turning, especially since it seemed to be a requirement for the way Granny and they were turning me slow and conscious. Marty had talked about the Sight all those times, and I had supposed, in the part of my mind that observed what was happening to me, that the Sight just made me vulnerable, maybe meant I'd See even more when I was on the other side. I'd never thought about that before, but then, I had a whole new perspective coming to me. There weren't so many people with the Sight as there were Reborn.

They weren't trying to cure the Reborn. They were trying to make them different, make them smart, keep them people.

It came as all cramped stomach and smell—I could smell everything, including the remnants of stew in the bowl and on the spoon, the honest sweat in Dell's creases and folds from a day outside, the washing powder they'd used in the sheets. And under that, a different smell, a broken one, something human that wasn't human anymore. I sniffed, deliberate about it. It was me. My own self, open pores and dead skin cells, a strand of hair on my pillowcase.

The shadows crept in then, the Sight that I'd expected to fill up my view, the room spinning around. And then I felt the smoothness of cloth under my cheek, unlike the roughness of the floor before. I sat up from the bed and everything stayed where it needed to be; the light seemed brighter and the weave of the sheet was crisp and clear. My vision focused on details out from there, like the edges of a dark blanket had been pulled back, revealing what I hadn't even known was covered up.

My field of vision was wider because the corners of my eyes were open. Dell wore jeans. The denim was faded and worn thin in patches, old and comfortable. Her hand, resting on the bed next to her thigh, was a network of skin and muscle and bone and blood vessels—I could see the tiny hairs on her arm, just a dust of fuzz. One of her cuticles was ragged. And as soft as her hands felt, she had the start of a callus on the middle finger of her right hand. I'd never seen her write, but it looked like she was able and did so frequently.

I knew so much about her just from looking, from Seeing her with my new eyes. My new living eyes. I hadn't even died, and I'd been Reborn. I thought for a split second about Seymour and that revival tent. He hadn't even known the truth of what he'd been preaching. I had a whole new life in my hands, in my guts, in all of my organs.

Dell had moved back when I sat up, and I leaned forward another little bit, sniffed again. She flinched back like she knew what I was doing and when I eased the covers back, forgetting how weak I'd been before she'd fed me, Dell moved away from me, across the wooden floor on her boot-covered feet. She would have traction, might be fast. Probably wouldn't slip and fall if I treated her like prey.

That stopped me the way her retreat wasn't able to—that thought of her like prey. But wasn't that what it meant to be turned, to be a Reborn? I was full now, but I'd need to eat again. I'd always need to eat again.

My feet were steady. I was barefooted, but that wouldn't slow me down none. If I wanted to, I could run. I could be fast and sure and certain. Instead of the old horror I'd felt remembering that Reborn in the woods, I wondered now if I could move like that. I suspected that I could, that I wouldn't give up when I was after something or someone. I wouldn't have to give up.

The floor creaked under me, and Dell backed herself up to the door. She twisted the knob, then twisted it again. The door was locked.

Her face lit up with panic; she hadn't just locked the door behind herself by accident. She'd brought herself in here as a good little nursemaid to feed me my breakfast, but she hadn't banked on being breakfast herself.

Of course, we all knew what you got for trusting banks. Nothing but empty promises and locked doors when it was time for them to give you what was yours. She didn't need to worry though, I'd give her what she deserved. With interest.

That wasn't a comforting thought—it was a thought I hadn't even known myself capable of thinking until that very moment. It was like something else thought it inside of my head, considered its next meal. But it was just me in there. "What kind of meat was in the stew?" I asked, and I already knew, but I wanted to make her say it, wanted her to admit what she'd done to me. Dell shook her head, jiggled the locked doorknob again, closer to frantic with every step I took.

Then I caught her gaze. That's how it had worked with the Reborn and that squirrel. He'd held it by the power of his Sight and even though the thing had jerked and pulled, its will wasn't strong enough and it had been tied up tight. Might as well have had a bow on its head like a present for all the freedom it'd had once that Reborn gotten it in his view. I could do that now, though it'd probably take practice to do it over long distances. Maybe it was easier with small things, but something told me big things were easy up close. Like people.

I could just about manage one girl over five feet. And then it was four feet. And then I didn't care about the distance because I was right up there in her face. I gave her a good smell, the fear coming off of her sweet neck. She had a long throat, with a beauty mark on one side. My mouth watered—hot saliva pooling under my tongue.

It would be easy. Whoever had locked her in was feeding her to me the same way she'd fed me stew, right to my mouth without a drop gone to waste. I tilted my head at that, at the memory of it—it was minutes ago, no matter how long it felt like I'd been holding down her willpower under the pressure of mine. I'd eaten. And I'd been full. Every time she'd fed me, I'd been full to the point of bursting.

So full that I wasn't hungry. I dropped the hand I'd halfway extended, nearly there to touching her cheek and grasping her hair. I could still be on her before she fought the compulsion. I could savor her and eat for pleasure.

"Get on out of here." I turned my eyes away, focused on the corner of the room, small and shadowed, hopeful she'd figure out how to unlock the door from where she was. The baseboards were the same red wood as the floors. Dell's sob was loud in my ear; louder still when she banged on the door and screamed for someone to let her out. I backed up, backed up until the mattress was at the backs of my knees and all the strength seemed to go right out of me until I fell back onto the covers. I closed my eyes.

The door opened, smooth on its hinges so there wasn't any noise, but I felt it open in the pressure of the air, wood swaying a breeze. Dell kept crying on her way out. Then the click of the lock again, secure and safe—though I wasn't sure right then if the idea was to keep me safe from whoever was out there or to keep them safe from me.

I wasn't real sure I even cared. With my eyes closed and my hands on my belly, I hummed to myself until I went back to sleep, a nap after a good meal. I'd think about the rest of it later.

CHAPTER SEVENTEEN

Some Choices Are Easier Than Others

I was still humming when I woke up again, the blanket under my fingers in shreds. I had to think hard about it to let the fabric go, but there was no confusion about where I was or what had happened, none of the dream state that had plagued me through the cycle of them feeding me. I had always been waking up because I had always been asleep. Now there was no gently lifting fog; there was a song from all of my senses that made me sit up and take notice.

The door was open.

I pushed all of the covers back—they were too warm, too confining. No sign of visitors since Dell had left; that was no surprise.

Nothing had been nearly as simple as I'd thought—I'd been set on surviving, so I hadn't stopped much to consider the bigger picture. That was Marty setting me out into the storm knowing that someone— probably the same people who'd killed my parents and her husband— would find me, and that was Dell picking me up and taking me deep inside the fence where I'd be sure to lose myself even if I didn't find myself subject to their job. Whatever they called it, they'd done their work on me for sure, fed me their tainted meat a little at a time just to see if it would be enough and when it was, they'd taken me the rest of the way to a new home, a new way of being. I hadn't had to die to rise again. I wasn't going to lose myself.

That big picture—the one where I hadn't noticed the lack of radios, but where everyone had their mail. The oddities about the buildings I had never tried to track down a reason for.

This wasn't a town for the living, at least not for the living alone. Without the Reborn, it wouldn't even exist. Or it'd exist the same way Wanton did, a little bit on the edge of everything where we all had tried to keep one step ahead of the dust. Near enough not to feel alone, but far enough to feel like we were on our own, like we weren't taking handouts.

Government Station 12 wasn't a town. It was an outpost. And while I didn't know all the details just yet, it was safe to think I knew some people who could tell me.

That startled me, the sureness that I could make people tell me anything I wanted. I'd never have assumed that kind of thing before and I wanted to be mad about it, wanted to scream at the people who'd turned me into a thing I'd been afraid of all my life. But I couldn't make that feeling happen, couldn't get riled up about it when it all seemed to be coming right out of my own head.

I thought about the stories we'd been told, about relatives getting gnawed up by new Reborn seeking them out, and I wondered. There was no way I was going to be the same person I always had been, but maybe I'd still be a little bit the same, at least until I wound up feral, wandering wherever my hunger took me. If I had to wind up feral. Maybe I didn't.

That damn Jimmy—that was what he'd meant. Him and Granny both, telling me I shouldn't ever go hungry. It was like a puzzle piece locking in, making sense out of what had seemed too random before. My instincts, the ones I had been so quick to dismiss before as being outrageous and paranoid, told me yes. And this time I listened, nodded along because instinct was going to be my most honest teacher.

Stretching felt good, felt better than any stretching I'd ever done before. I was ready to move, and I knew the power behind my joints. Those wooden beams weren't decorative; this was stronger than my little room, the coop they'd kept me safe in while I laid eggs for them.

This was on the other side of the blue door that had held my attention. This was a feeding house.

The name seemed right, no matter what anyone else would call the place. This was where they fed the folk they were turning after they'd starved them down to nothing in the station. Other things went on there, I didn't know for sure what, but I bet the starving happened there. That boy was starving there right now, but I was already turned, already fed to fullness, a successful experiment different from that boy, whether the folks in the station knew it or not. I'd been hungry in the woods, been going without for longer than ever had been necessary in my life. But I didn't think that was the important part; I didn't think the starving was actually needed. And somehow, Granny had known that, had hit on the part that *was* needed: feeding me up with flesh until it was the only thing in me. She'd known how to make me without unmaking me first. And I'd been Marty's sacrifice for it.

I stood up and my own naked skin caught me off guard. I'd gotten rid of my rank nightgown at some point or someone had taken it off me before tucking me into that bed. There was no telling—except I probably could figure it out if I spent some time sniffing around. I had never been one to take my clothes off in the middle of the night, much less in my sleep.

But I'd also never felt this rumble in my stomach, like if I didn't eat, I was going to go right out of my head with it. Food was more important than clothes then. It was hard to hold on to any idea of why they'd be important the more I thought about my hunger. Now that I was aware of it, the throb drowned everything else out. I frowned, but the rub of my lips on my teeth distracted me from whatever had seemed wrong about the situation.

I stumbled to the door, not nearly as sure on my feet as I'd been earlier, earlier when I'd been looking at food. My thighs slid past each other, and I managed to rush out the door and into the room beyond. White walls, bright light, clean floors. Nothing to eat. I kept moving, focused on my balance, and it came easier with every step. Earlier— earlier when I had thought about eating Dell. I crossed the room to the door without making a conscious decision to do so. If I'd thought about it, I'd have figured the door for locked. I'd have been wrong.

No one around, at least none that were accessible, and wasn't that a smart precaution if they were just letting a hungry Reborn roam their streets? I didn't smell people or hear them. It was all chickens. Just the chickens. I'd felt bad at some point that the blue door opened up onto a chicken coop. I'd thought how smelly a front yard that would make. Now, my feet leading me down the two rough steps, it seemed like the best possible arrangement. Breakfast right outside my front door.

The birds clucked, used to my presence every morning to the point that my evening arrival didn't startle them. But when I got closer, the big silver hen who'd been one of my best layers rucked up her head and looked at me, beady eye focused from further away than she should have been able to see. The same power rose in me that I'd used on Dell—I could keep her still, hold all those birds still until I made it through the fence. She'd be raw but fresh, and I was so hungry.

Before I could try to hold her, she clucked like the biddy she was, shied back from the extended beak of another bird that was rushing at her. They had neat and tidy chicken yard claws, nothing like the old fighting roosters I'd seen in town years before—no knives strapped to their legs neither—but I still flinched back in some echo of sympathy. The body of the other bird made a dull solid thump against her breast, sent her skittering across the dirt. It wasn't normal, and it had broken my eye contact before I'd had a chance to latch on.

Rocks ground under a boot sole and I turned, fast and overbalanced, so braced for an impact that I nearly lost my footing on the dirt. Jimmy, always shirtless Jimmy with his shoulders and his freckles, walked on careful feet, hands raised like they'd be any barrier between us. He'd be even easier than Dell—he wanted to try my mouth out for kissing, and he'd stand there for it until it was too late for him.

I was on the balls of my feet, leaning forward, when Jimmy turned his head away, refused to look at me, opened his mouth. "Hank— Henrietta Goodness, you better stop. You'd best stop that right now."

It caught me off guard; there was no way for him to know my full name like that. I hadn't told anyone, that much I'd kept in my mouth. Yet, somehow he'd still known who I was, maybe this whole time.

I couldn't find my own voice, could only stand back on my heels and watch him like he was doing something interesting though I couldn't quite tell what. This didn't feel like a reaction I'd give, but I was getting used to it just the same.

"Henrietta, you come with me. Leave those chickens alone—I've got something else for you, just follow me easy." Every time he used my name, though it wasn't as good as my nickname, there was a lurch in my chest, like my lungs stood up and hitched their pants back into place before heading out the door. "Come on now, I know you're hungry."

He was right about that. When he took a step back, I took a step forward. He made it nice and slow and easy, like he was afraid I'd bolt though I didn't know if that meant away or toward him. But he kept me following him until we reached a door that seemed familiar and I recognized it with my new eyes—Granny's kitchen. I'd sat in there, ate in there, cooked in there. The smell of it caught at my nose, led me in across the threshold by my nostrils until Jimmy pointed at a chair just waiting for me. There was a place set with a bowl and silverware and a glass full of clear water.

Jimmy had clean hands, no dirt under his fingernails, just like Dell. That should have been a clue—Ben and I had been filthy for years, sandy grey topsoil ground into my nail beds for as long as I could remember. My cuticles stayed raggedy under my teeth, too, when I was stressed or just not paying attention.

My hands went for the bowl and I caught myself—there was a spoon there. And a chair. I pulled it back and made myself slow down for enough heartbeats. I could sit and eat. I'd done it before. The scrape of the wooden legs as I pulled the chair out caught at my ears—loud and jarring—but it wasn't enough to drive me away. I sat like I had last time, my body remembering even if my brain was catching back up, distracted by all the new information.

Even though I stared at the bowl in front of me, I could tell Jimmy hovered, traded off glances between the door we'd come in through and the door that led further into the house. Watched for someone.

"Eat it all, Hank, hell, eat it up." He rubbed his hands down the long length of his denim-clad thighs.

I'd been getting closer to those chickens, ready to cross that fence like it wasn't there, but for some reason I couldn't take a bite of whatever he served until he'd told me to do it. It wasn't that I needed his permission. He'd just surprised me enough that I wasn't sure what I was supposed to do, instincts or no. And he'd used my full name, my real true name, back out there in the yard, like he knew me from a long time ago.

Henrietta Goodness—even Marty didn't call me that. If he'd used my middle name, I might have died right there on the spot. Ben might not have even known my middle name, or if he did, he might have forgotten it by the time we were old enough to know not to spread them around. I lifted the spoon and dug into the stew, another one of Granny's endless stews she poured down everyone's gullet.

But I'd assumed that about everything else I'd eaten, too, that I was eating the same thing everyone else was, and look where that had got me. "What is it?" My voice rasped, like it had been in hibernation.

Those shoulders slumped in something that could only be relief. "I was worried for a hot minute there." His hands eased to his sides, and Jimmy inhaled deep enough to sigh. "It's deer—deer I shot myself." When I kept eating, he moved to the other side of the table and found his own seat. "I made the stew, too."

He'd killed it and made it for me. No chance of it being tainted then. I appreciated the reassurance though I wondered if he'd meant it in any other fashion. "Bit late on the draw for that, isn't it?" Wasn't I already changed and hungrier than I'd ever been, even hungrier than when Dell had led me in through the gate?

Jimmy's mouth wasn't meant to sneer, but his lips curled and he made a good effort at it. "Hank, I swear you don't think with a lick of sense even when someone hands you the damn answers." He pushed further back from the table, frustration in that wood-on-wood squeal. "You don't listen worth anything."

That was anger, real anger and a little bit of fear that I could taste on the back of my tongue. It was like a sauce for my stew. I raised my head to savor it before I could stop myself. With food in my mouth though, my stomach didn't scream at me anymore. "You don't even talk all that much."

Something creaked in the innards of the house—Jimmy twitched toward the sound, braced, but nobody came rushing in and he relaxed one muscle at a time. When he snorted, he sounded like a horse clearing its nose of dust. "You think talking's easy in a place like this?"

That might have been the most honest thing I'd heard anyone inside the fence—inside Government Station 12—say. I chewed the bite of food in my mouth, went over it and over it again with my teeth. There were other stations. Probably doing the same thing. "You're trying to find a cure?" That fit with Marty's story, too, about the government always working on its secret cure.

The eye roll he gave me in response made me choke. I winced back from taking another mouthful. Winced again when I got gravy on my chin. Jimmy was right—I hadn't been paying attention. "You make them— us—here. You make people Reborn." Another thought surprised me, and this time, I bit my tongue trying to force it out. "Are you Reborn?"

I didn't think he'd be able to hide something like that from me so his headshake was no particular surprise. I had some notion that like would recognize like.

"No, you don't smell right." That was what it was. Though that wasn't a sentence I'd ever expected to find myself on the giving end of. Still, it was the truth, just as much as me sitting there feeling more human by the minute. I put my spoon down in my near-empty bowl and unclenched my fingers from their white-knuckle grip around it. "That's what Granny meant when she said I should eat. She really meant I should eat."

My memory of the Reborn in the woods, desperate bony fingers digging into the body of the captured squirrel, was as clear as the day I'd seen him, but now those sharp edges took on a different meaning, cut me like teeth. That was the difference. He was feral. He'd gone hungry, too hungry, and lost everything. I didn't have to be like them. I could have been—the way that chicken had looked at me made me think I'd been pretty close—but I wasn't.

"You're getting there." Jimmy stood up, reached for my bowl, but did it slowly and carefully.

That was how I recognized the growl rising in my throat without thought—I stuffed it back down and let him clear my place. Clearly, I needed to keep myself fed, needed to pay attention to my body's opinions. If other people felt like food, I would need to watch myself or I'd treat them like food—the way I'd treated Dell. There was no room to slip—or I'd be no better than that ragged skeleton.

I stopped, held my breath, and closed my eyes, and just stopped. My heart kept on with its beating, and my lungs waited for what I was going to do next. The house made its usual every day settling noises. My skin tingled with it—air currents blowing around, and the vibration of just having another person close by. The wood of the floor was smooth under my feet, worn by a hundred other people sitting there before me.

Also, I was still naked. Which made Jimmy's refusal to look anywhere but at my face or away from me make a lot more sense.

"I need some clothes." I pulled myself closer to the table, hunched lower. I'd forgotten—hadn't given it half a thought once I'd had food in front of me. My stomach had taken over. And Jimmy had been worried I was going to after him, he really had. Now that I could breathe again, I could read the look that had been on his face. Not so much fear as the worry he was going to have to put me down.

At least Jimmy wasn't helpless, but there was room in me to be glad he hadn't had to take that option. And gladder still he handed me a bundle of fabric from a bag he'd had slung across his back. I hadn't even seen it. That was another thing to look out for then—keeping my eyes on the whole garden plot instead of just one row.

Somewhere, I didn't even care where or how, he'd dug up a pair of old jeans that looked like they would fit me. I pulled them up my legs under the table. No underwear, but I could live without that, especially since the denim was soft and clean. There was a bra, one that had probably been filched from the wash I'd sent down, and a white undershirt, stained a little yellow under the arms. He blushed when I looked at him, and I realized this was one of his shirts that he never wore. I elbowed my way into it, tucked the bra in the front pocket of my new jeans. Reborn or not, there was no way I was putting that on in front of him.

There were socks but no shoes. Jimmy had turned, and I didn't think he'd be the kind to sneak a peek, but he was listening, straining to hear like he'd caught a warning. Maybe he had. I heard it then—footsteps and the light sound of Dell's laughter. It sounded like vinegar. She swung open the door from inside the house, the one I had always taken to get to my room, and stopped with her laugh dead in the air between us. I shoved my other foot into the second sock and was on my feet. Dell looked away from me.

I knew from that she did remember being in the feeding room with me. She remembered, and I could feel it between my legs just as much as I could feel it in my belly, the way she'd trembled like a hunted creature. That, and she was still working with Martin. Him and Granny, too, because Granny had to be involved, had offered her up as a sacrifice to me, like she was nothing but stew in a bowl. What had they told her or promised her to make her stay instead of running away? Was there anyplace she could even run to that would be safe?

He was behind her; Martin didn't pretend to smile, didn't pause. He rushed forward, hands grabbing, trying to catch me by my hair. I ducked out of his way, under the table, faster than I thought I would be but still caught in the kitchen. Jimmy stood, tried to get in his way, but Martin shoved him until Jimmy fell away, shoulder hitting the floor with the brutal sound of flesh on wood. My vision narrowed, and all I saw was the space around me and the way Martin's muscles bunched before they launched him in a new direction. I waited, one breath, two breaths, and I watched. I leapt away from the direction he was broadcasting, but it wasn't anything I'd ever had to do before, and I was slower than I should have been. My socked feet caught against a table leg, and I stumbled.

CHAPTER EIGHTEEN

What Cannot Be Cured Must Be Endured

atch her, goddamnit, catch her." Martin was loud enough that other people would hear, would come running. I stood up fast and tried to push the table toward him, but it was old and heavy enough that I just crashed myself backward into the wall. The chair rail caught me across the small of my back and I flinched from the pain, not sure I could use my legs for an instant.

Dell was circling, wary but willing. Even Jimmy had crouched, back on his feet though he favored his arm. His body shouted he'd jump me if I tried to make it past him, but his eyes held a different message. Dell was afraid of me, had never had any real fondness for me no matter how I mooned after her, and she looked like a fighter in a ring. Jimmy had come for me, fed me, believed in me. I made my choice, rushed toward him—and he stepped aside, a silent agreement.

I wasn't the only one to see it though—Martin sprang after me and caught me by the wrist, grinding the bones together sudden enough that my feet jerked out from under me. He followed me to the ground, heavier than he looked as I bucked and struggled. "Get Dr. Travers." Dell took off, but Jimmy inched closer. "Don't even think it, Junior. I'll deal with you later." Jimmy's stubborn face was pale, but his eyes narrowed—he saw it for the threat it was. He barreled into Martin, and they rolled off me in a heap of struggling limbs. I sprang up, scuttled away like a crab—if I was getting out of here, I had to take Jimmy with me now. I owed him that, but I had to figure out how.

Jimmy was quicker on his feet than Martin; he wriggled away from where Martin furiously grappled for him and jumped up off the floor. He took a wary wrestler's stance and then thought better of it. Jimmy jerked out of the way before I grabbed for whatever I could—the pot of stew always bubbling on the stove—and hurled it at Martin where he had made it to his knees. The simmering stew and heavy pot got his attention, and that was all I could do, there was no time for shoes or saying goodbyes. I wore my mother's ring and that was all that I had that was *mine*. I dashed outside, Jimmy behind me with his bag slung over his back again.

And then I listened, realized I was as foolish as Jimmy had said—I opened my ears and Listened. Dell had gone for Granny, who I realized *was* Dr. Travers. I could hear Dell's running feet, but everyone else had stayed away, waiting to see the result of the experiment, waiting to find out if the turning would take and if I'd go feral or stay aware of myself. I bet I knew where they had hidden themselves, too, trying to keep safe.

Jimmy shoved me, and I realized I'd stopped moving. "Head for the gate. We can get out that way." He kept pushing until I started to move again.

There were worse choices I could make than trusting him, so once I got my feet unstuck, I ran for it with him hot behind me, leaving that building behind in the center of town even though part of me wanted to go and burn it down before we left, before we made our escape into the dusk. They all hid there, behind its white walls, busily tinkering with their experiments. I didn't want to be another one of them anymore. But there was no time, not unless I wanted Martin to get ahold of me for real this time and not let go. There couldn't be any good ending to that when I didn't have a plan, wasn't sure enough of what I could do or how to do it.

Even as I ran, though, half-formed plans distracted me; we could come back, we would come back. There was no way the government would shut down a place like this, it was too involved to run a whole station like this. Granny had talked about her job—they'd all stay here working at it no matter what, and we could come back and fix things. That kid I'd seen Martin drag in there, I promised him I'd come back when I could, no matter what state he was in.

And then Jimmy was slowing me before we reached the gate, before the guards could turn and notice us. He steered me around a corner, under a deep shadow cast by the roof overhang. The socks I'd put on were already filthy on the bottom with dirt; it ground into the soles of my feet. Jimmy whispered, voice next to my ear. "You have to freeze them—like you did with Dell when you were hungry."

So he knew about that. Had he helped me because of it or in spite of it? Had she told him or did he find out on his own? Maybe he'd been there, the one to lock the door on the other side of her. But I'd wanted Dell. Wanted to feel her in my mouth and under my hands. I didn't know how to do that with these strangers who I'd worked so hard to make familiar—they had avoided eye contact with me the whole time, and now I knew why. This wasn't going to work; we were going to be trapped inside the fence.

"Hank, come on." Jimmy was starting to sound desperate, like the look on my face told him everything he needed to know. Like he was starting to regret the risk he was taking.

These guards, the way they'd held their guns so easily and kept their gaze unfocused. I had to try to hear them, keep my ears open wide, because they kept their stillness and their watch. They were in the habit of turning to scan inside the fence, too—and now I wondered if it was to rest their eyes from all the looking they did outside. So they were probably already relaxing when they turned to face in—believing everything inside was well contained—and focusing up again when they turned to face out.

It was a lot of supposing. But it fit what I'd seen and how I'd never been able to meet their eyes before—I tried at the wrong time.

This was the wrong time now, too, with everything riding on me being able to catch and hold them when I'd only been able to do that with Dell before. They didn't even turn at the same time, which made sense from a not leaving the gate undefended perspective. "I can't grab both of them." I braced for Jimmy's disappointment.

Instead, he just nodded. "All right then, I'll take care of Robbie—he's the one on the left." He didn't look happy about it, shoulders square and big hands flexing. "You grab Nelson, and when Robbie turns to figure out what's going on, I'll knock him out."

As precarious a plan as it sounded, at least it was a plan that got us outside without hurting anyone too bad. I took a couple of deep breaths, trying to figure out what I'd done when I'd held onto that chicken. I needed to be able to freeze a whole person and do it deliberately, make them stick where they stood just by the force of my willpower alone.

I'd never had very much of that, or maybe just never exercised it, content with running around and mostly doing whatever Marty wanted. I stood up to Ben, but he was my brother, and I'd always given in eventually, when he was hurt or even just pretended to be. Doing that had led me here, and there was no way of knowing what would be happening instead if I'd made my own path. I'd been easy prey in more ways than one, but I was learning different now. You didn't have to have the Sight to be Reborn—but I had that, and I had my will. And I could use both of those things.

Before the first guard turned—Nelson, Jimmy had called him—I waited, still and silent like I'd been at the kitchen table and caught my breath in my chest. Granny hadn't seen me then and Nelson wouldn't see me now if I went about things the right way. I moved slow, careful out from the shadows. It had been the sound of the chair, that sharp protesting squeal of a wooden leg on a wooden floor, that had made Granny and Jimmy startle. That Reborn in the woods moved without noise, and my bones whispered I could do it easily. They were eager for me to try. All of me was eager. I let my foot rest lightly in front of me before I settled my weight on it, testing each patch of ground to make sure it wouldn't betray my presence. My socks weren't doing me any favors, but I didn't have time to take them off.

When I'd needed to get away, I'd done much the same thing; my knees had been lucky in the rich black soil, but I'd felt that stick under me and moved my weight away from it. I hadn't thought much about the trick at the time, but I concentrated now, focused on the leaves and dirt and wood chips under the sole of my foot.

And when Nelson turned, I stood in front of him. His eyes were unfocused, and I was still, so still, with my heart and my breathing so soft and even and quiet, they would have rocked me to sleep if I'd been a baby in a cradle. I let my eyelids droop the same way his were and kept my attention on the movement of Nelson's lungs, watched him expand as he drew in a breath until, finally, his gaze sharpened.

I opened my eyes, no wider than usual, but I opened them, and I Looked at him, the way I'd caught Dell, so that all he could see was me, so that he couldn't look away or shout out. I didn't feel desirous about him; there was no slick of want under my tongue. But my stomach took notice anyway, and he was caught even tighter. I stepped closer, sniffed like I could smell him: salt and something bitter, burnt coffee gone cold.

Something told me he wouldn't taste very good until I got inside, until I got into the meat of him. But I stopped myself from following that thought—I wasn't doing anything but holding him still. And then it was hard to do that; he struggled, and even his arms twitched. The guards had to have had some training, had to have willpower of their own.

The sudden fight of it tightened my gut, and my teeth ground in the back of my jaw. There was no way I was letting him go. It didn't matter if I didn't want him; he was mine just the same and fighting against it wasn't any way for him to survive. In fact, the more he struggled, the tighter I held on, my feet creeping me further forward without me making any conscious decisions about it. I tried to shake off the compulsion to pull him totally under, but when I wavered and tried to loosen my hold, he fought back until I clamped back down.

There had to be a balance, a way to keep him frozen without risking his life and my own willingness to do things I wouldn't when I wasn't just acting on my new instincts. When I was still my thinking self. I'd practice, I promised myself I'd practice, and in the meantime, I held on for all I was worth both to Nelson and to my own hands even though my feet had brought me right up in front of him.

A body dropped beside me, and then Nelson dropped, too; I whirled to defend my catch, and Jimmy held his fists balled up together. He shook them out like his hands hurt. They must have, and for a second, I felt like that was an injury I should exploit. Jimmy stepped back and checked behind us; there was nothing between us and outside the fence. "Come on." He grabbed my arm and hauled me out into the dusk. I concentrated on how strong his grip was and shoved my instincts down deep.

It was easy to cross the threshold of the fence. Not sure what I expected once we slipped out, but the woods looked the same as they had when I'd gone inside the fence with Dell. I was the one who was different this time, and Jimmy didn't seem afraid either. He hurried me along, but I followed under my own power and marked the direction he was taking me. North. North and a little east, toward the city, or at least toward the train. I wouldn't argue with that unless I found reason to—I was pointed in the direction of Ben again, and that felt correct despite all of Marty's warnings. I was already turned. That gave me an advantage.

There was no reason to hesitate; the dusk held no danger anymore. It was going to be cooler in the dark, and the light was going to be beautiful once the moon came out.

And behind us, swelled the shouting of frustrated people, some of whom I knew, some of whom I had fed lunch in the hot afternoons at Granny's table. Had their prophet foreseen any of this, had realized I would run? I moved faster; I didn't want to leave Jimmy behind, but my legs wanted to stretch, wanted to leave those voices far outpaced so they didn't pose any danger. They wouldn't join us in the darkness; they were too afraid for that.

But they'd know how to hunt me, know how to put me down like a horse with a broken leg, especially since I wasn't very strong yet. They might not have a cure, but they had all my weaknesses down in their papers because they'd been the ones to give them to me. They were there to do experiments, and I was just another one of them—I couldn't have been the first. Jimmy might be a help with that, might be able to tell me what they hadn't taught me. But first, we had to get away.

Jimmy swore and stumbled, fell to his side, and I remembered that he couldn't see as well in the dark. "Why'd you help me?" I had a hand extended to help him up, but I kept my fingers just out of his reach, waiting for a response.

He shook his head from where he sprawled on the ground. "It's not right. None of it is. But you did what they asked, and they turned you anyway, just because they wanted to see if they could."

Just because I was the right kind of person and I'd fallen into their laps, more like. If even that had been an accident, if Marty hadn't done it on purpose. They took advantage of what was brought to them, just like any other hunter. I didn't want to be like them, not if I could help it. I leaned down to offer Jimmy my hand.

There wasn't anything there now, but it would be soon enough: a rumble, deep in my gut. I'd need to eat. That's what Granny and Jimmy tried to tell me—and when I really considered it, that's what Marty had been telling me my whole life. There was no need to go hungry. I'd take my meals where I could find them and make them out of whatever was at hand because otherwise I'd lose myself and I'd lose Jimmy, too. Right between my teeth, I'd lose him. And that would cost me everything— any hope of finding Ben.

Going hungry would cost me myself and my body, and I'd wind up like that revenant of a human I'd first seen in a cage under that tent.

That was my new goal, the hope Marty had denied me when she'd put me out of the house. And maybe she'd been right, in a way. Maybe whoever had taken my brother would have eaten me up without thinking twice about it before. But now I was more than I had been, and what we called them, what we called *us* meant something different. I really had been Reborn, on the other side of that break in my lifeline with my self still intact.

His hand was warm in mine, strong, as he used me as leverage to stand up. It put him right up close to me again and he looked at my mouth like he still thought it might best be used for kissing instead of eating. I stepped back, and he let the space grow between us, didn't say a word.

There'd be time for that conversation. Time to find out how he'd known my name and whether or not I should trust him with more than getting me out of that station. I hadn't asked how he'd wound up there, but I would. And he'd probably tell me the truth. For now, I gestured for him to turn around and lead us away. I stayed behind him long enough to put on the bra that I had tucked into my pocket; it had stayed put not only through the scuffle with Martin, but when Jimmy and I made our break through the gate. The laughter was a relief even though I couldn't remember the last time I'd found something so damn funny.

Jimmy looked back over his shoulder at me, and I waved him off. I was okay. Everything was surprisingly okay, and if I could just remember that, then I could keep control of myself.

I'd never seen a map, but I knew what the land was like north of Wanton, north of here—Florida prairie, covered with grasses and short, tough bushes. Rumor had it there were still bison there and horses during the dry season. It was always the dry season but, as the air started to prickle with the electricity that came before thunder, I wondered if that was going to hold true.

That Reborn in the woods, all bones and rags, sprang to my mind. I rubbed my own fingers together. I wasn't like that. And I didn't have to be. So maybe it would finally rain after all these years, and maybe Jimmy and I had a hell of a long walk ahead of us. But I had every confidence we could make it, a positive feeling sitting warm and foreign in my chest.

ABOUT THE AUTHOR

Marianne Kirby writes about bodies both real and imagined. She plays with the liminal space between vanishing and visibility: she thinks the things that go bump in the night need to spend some time in the sun.

A long-time writer, editor, and activist, Marianne is a frequent contributor to women's interest  publications, news outlets, and tv shows that require people to have opinions. She has been published by the Guardian, xoJane, the Daily Dot, Bitch Magazine, Time, and others. She has appeared on tv and radio programs ranging from the Dr. Phil Show to Radio New Zealand.

Marianne was born in Florida and returned there because Florida Weird calls to its own. She has briefly escaped again but is already plotting her eventual winter migration.

This is her first novel.

Thank You
for Reading

http://mariannekirby.com

Please visit http://curiosityquills.com/reader-survey to share
your reading experience with the author of this book!

The Summer The World Ended, by Matthew S. Cox

Riley McCullough thinks it's the end of the world when her best friend gets 'dragged' off to Puerto Vallarta for the first two weeks of summer vacation—at least until the bombs fall. Her life turns upside down when she's forced to move across the country to live with a father she hasn't seen in six years, in a town where everyone distrusts them. Things seem better when she meets a boy who shares her video game hobby, but nuclear Armageddon threatens to take away everything she has left.

Broken Dolls, by Tyrolin Puxty

Ella doesn't remember what it's like to be human – after all, she's lived as a doll for thirty years. She forgets what it's like to taste, to smell...to breathe. The professor's obsession with turning sickly girls into dolls is starting to mess with Ella's head – and it's time for her to break free.

Homunculus & The Cat, by Nathan Croft

In a world where every culture's mythology is real, Medusa's sisters want revenge on Poseidon, Troy is under siege again, and the Yakuza want their homunculi (mythological artificial humans) back. Near Atlantis' Chinatown, a kitten and her human campaign for homunculi rights. Against them are Japanese death gods, an underworld cult, and a fat Atlantean bureaucrat. The main character dies (more than once) and a few underworlds' way of death is threatened. Also with giant armored battle squids

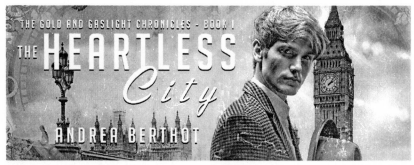

The Heartless City, by Andrea Berthot

It's 1903, and London has been quarantined for thirteen years, terrorized by a race of monsters created by Henry Jekyll. Due to his own devastating brush with science, seventeen-year-old Elliot is now an empath, leveled by the emotions of a terrorized, dying city. He finds an unlikely ally in a music hall waitress named Iris, and together they must discover who's pulling the strings in Jekyll's wake. Monsters, it turns out, are not the greatest evil they must face.

CPSIA information can be obtained
at www.ICGtesting.com
Printed in the USA
FSOW02n0702211216
28763FS